KU-215-069

BLOWBACK

Riley "Bear" Logan Book TWO

L.T. RYAN

Liquid Mind Media, LLC

Copyright © 2018 by L.T. Ryan and Liquid Mind Media, LLC. All rights reserved. No part of this publication may be copied, reproduced in any format, by any means, electronic or otherwise, without prior consent from the copyright owner and publisher of this book. This is a work of fiction. All characters, names, places and events are the product of the author's imagination or used fictitiously.

Jack Noble™ and The Jack Noble Series™ are trademarks of L.T. Ryan and Liquid Mind Media, LLC.

For information contact:

ltryan70@gmail.com

http://LTRyan.com

https://www.facebook.com/JackNobleBooks

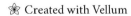 Created with Vellum

Dedication

Special thanks to Amy, Barbara, Don, Ed, George, Karen, Karen, Melissa, and Marty.
And thank you to all of the Jack Noble and Riley "Bear" Logan fans out there! I can not express the gratitude I have for your support. I'm still amazed every day when I wake up and "go to work" with these guys.
If, by chance, this story is your introduction to the world of Jack & Bear, get your chores and work done now, then strap in, and hang on for the ride. It's a wild one!
~L.T.

The Jack Noble Series

The Recruit (free)
The First Deception (Prequel 1)
Noble Beginnings
A Deadly Distance
Ripple Effect (Bear Logan)
Blowback (Bear Logan)
Thin Line
Noble Intentions
When Dead in Greece
Noble Retribution
Noble Betrayal
Never Go Home
Beyond Betrayal (Clarissa Abbot)
Noble Judgment
Never Cry Mercy
Deadline
End Game

Receive a free copy of The Recruit by visiting http://ltryan.com/newsletter.

Chapter One

Bear turned his face toward the sun as he strolled along the familiar path to the bar that had become his second home over the past six weeks. There's nothing quite like the Caribbean sun. It's a little warmer, a little more rejuvenating. Even after two months on St. Lucia, Bear wasn't used to how good the sun felt on his skin.

A foghorn in the distance brought Bear out of his peaceful reflection. As much as he enjoyed the weather and the food, St. Lucia was far from perfect. It was the height of tourist season, with three or four cruise liners pulling up to the coast every day. If he saw one more bad T-shirt, like *I can't keep calm, I'm going on a cruise*, he was going to jump into the ocean and swim until he drowned or some colossal sea creature decided to have him for dinner.

But not everything about St. Lucia was awful. The locals were patient with the tourists—it was their way of life, after all—but they didn't mind raising an eyebrow behind a few backs. They did their job and they did it well, but they never forgot that they were on constant display, living here in paradise. They all had to put up

1

with plenty of bullshit, but it's what kept their sense of humor so sharp.

Bear swung open the door to his local haunt. He'd visited plenty of bars in that first week, but the atmosphere at The Soggy Dollar was exactly what he had been looking for. They had great food, cheap beer, and a barmaid who didn't take lip from anyone. But the best part? The tourists didn't typically venture out this far.

Before Bear even reached his usual stool at the opposite end of the bar, there was a full glass of the local brew in front of him. He couldn't even remember the name of it, but it didn't matter. Sophia always seemed to know what he wanted even before he did.

Sophia leaned in close, a smirk on her face. "I saw a new one today."

Bear groaned. They'd been trading sightings of terrible T-shirts for the past week and Sophia was on a winning streak. "Do I even want to know?"

"Oh yeah," she said. "This one is even worse than *My guns aren't going to be the only thing that's out in St. Lucia.*"

Bear rolled his eyes. "We agreed that is not the worst one we've seen. It's not even funny."

"No, you agreed it's not the worst one we've seen. I agreed that you're just too old to get it."

"Too old, my ass," Bear said, but he took a sip of his beer to hide his smile. "So, lay it on me."

"Okay." Sophia flipped her long braids over her shoulder and put her hands out, setting the scene. "I was on my way to work and I see this old guy coming toward me, right?"

"How old? Not-actually-old like me or actually old like Dennis?" Bear hooked his thumb over his shoulder at the old-timer sitting at a table by himself on the other side of the bar. He had to be at least ninety.

Sophia scowled. She hated when he interrupted her stories. Which is exactly why he did it. "In between. Anyway, so I see this sweet old guy walking toward me, right? He's got a little hat on and khaki shorts and socks pulled up to his knees. He just looks happy to be here. So I smile at him and start to wave. And then I see his shirt."

Sophia paused. When Bear didn't say anything, she quirked an eyebrow. This was a pre-determined break in her story, the only point at which he was actually allowed to interrupt. He played along.

"What did it say?"

Sophia swept her hand out in front of her like she was imagining the words in shining lights hovering in front of her face. *"Can I try your fish taco?"*

Bear blinked once. Then twice. He didn't know what to say.

Sophia threw up her hands. "I don't even know why I bother."

"Maybe he just really loves fish tacos?"

"I'm sure he does, but that bastard Randolph at the corner shop sells them to college students who think they're hilarious because they have the maturity of a twelve-year-old boy." She shook her head. "That poor man. Everyone is gonna be laughing at him. He has no idea."

Bear pretended to be affronted. "You mean you didn't say anything to save that poor soul's dignity?"

"I couldn't do that to him! He looked so happy." Sophia got a wicked grin on her face. "But I did give Randolph a piece of my mind."

Bear chuckled. "I'm sure you did. He'll be feeling that for a week."

Sophia just shrugged. "He's forgotten what it means to be from St. Lucia. All he cares about is the money."

"The world needs more people like you, Sophia."

"The world needs more people like us, Bear."

Sophia smiled, but Bear didn't return the gesture. No one knew who he was here, and he wanted to keep it that way. He only had a handful of acquaintances. He counted Sophia and her fiancé, Derek, as friends, but they didn't know the real Riley Logan. As far as they were aware, he was just some rich guy from the States who decided to get away for a while. He didn't offer up any explanations and they didn't ask questions.

The only problem was that Sophia seemed privy to the fact that Bear did have some secrets. She never pried, but sometimes she looked at him like she knew he'd been through the wringer. Usually she'd just give him a beer on the house, but sometimes he saw pity in her eyes. That's usually when he'd crack a joke at her expense, lighting up that fire inside her that always bubbled right under the surface. She'd forget about any sympathy she had for him and spend the rest of the night berating him, much to the delight of the other locals. That, at least, he could handle.

The creak of the door broke the silence forming between him and the barmaid. Bear, who refused to keep the door at his back, was first to see Derek enter. Sophia finished pouring a beer for one of the other customers before looking up. A giant grin spread across her face.

If Sophia was fire, then Derek was the coolest, calmest waters on St. Lucia. Bear had never seen him get angry once, and he was the only person on the island who could talk Sophia out of one of her rampages.

Derek slid onto the stool next to Bear and greeted him by way of clapping him on the shoulder. Then he turned to his fiancé and flashed her a grin of his own. "*Bonjour, mon ange.*"

"Don't you *mon ange* me, Derek Arthur Lewis. You're late." Sophia tried to sound tough, but she couldn't keep the sparkle out of her eyes. She'd recently confided in Bear that she was pregnant, making him promise not to say anything to Derek. She wanted to wait until after the wedding.

"I would've been here sooner, but I ran into Randolph on the way over."

If Sophia was capable of shame, she would've looked sheepish. "I'm not apologizing to that man."

"Apparently you scared away a dozen of his customers." Derek looked a little proud, but he was trying to hide it under an admonishing frown.

Sophia waved away the comment. "Five, if that. Anyway, he deserved it." She eyed Derek up and down. "What did you say to him?"

Derek shrugged. It was such a languid, peaceful movement when he did it. "I said if he wanted an apology he'd have to ask you for one himself."

"I'm not apologizing to that man."

"He knows that as well as I do, *mon ange*." Derek leaned forward across the bar and kissed Sophia on the cheek. "What's for lunch today?"

"You'll see." Sophia waved them both away. "Go get a table. *Go*. I'll bring it out shortly."

Bear and Derek swung around and spotted an empty table in the middle of the room. This was Bear's daily routine now. Wake up at dawn and walk around the island, taking in the sunrise and the bustle of activity that came with it. He'd read and explore and eat and watch, then visit The Soggy Dollar and have lunch with Derek.

Derek was a businessman by trade. He owned a half dozen tiny shops all over the island, managing each one with care and attention. Need a boat to go around the bay? Call Derek Lewis. Did your car break down? Call Derek Lewis. Found a snake in your toilet? Call Derek Lewis. It was a wonder the man had any time to sit down to a meal with Bear these days.

But there was an ulterior motive here. For the past two weeks Derek had been trying to get Bear to join him. Bear made the mistake of volunteering to help Derek for the day when one of his men called out sick. The two of them had sped through that day's work in half the time, and Derek had been asking Bear to join his crew ever since.

But Bear wasn't interested. St. Lucia was beautiful, to be sure. He had made a little life here under the warm comfort of the sun. He had found relaxation much more quickly than he would've thought possible after everything that went down in Costa Rica. But this wasn't home. And it never would be.

Bear had started to feel that itch under his skin in the last couple of days. He had tried his best to ignore it, but it refused to let up. He knew what it meant. It was almost time to move on. He was trying to draw it out for as long as possible, but he didn't think he'd make it until Sophia and Derek's wedding. Part of him wanted to just get up and go without telling them, if only to avoid Sophia's ire. But he knew he'd never be able to live with himself if he didn't say goodbye.

"Bear?" Derek's voice sounded like it was a thousand miles away. "Bear? Are you okay?"

"Yeah, yeah." Bear cleared his throat and looked up at Derek, who appeared genuinely concerned. Bear laughed. "I'm good. Just got lost in my thoughts there for a minute."

Derek bobbed his head up and down but didn't say anything. Bear got the impression that, just like his fiancé, Derek saw past many of Bear's defenses. He might not know anything about Bear's past, but he certainly had his suspicions. Bear was just grateful the man hadn't felt the need to come out and ask him about it. He'd never be able to tell either one of them the truth, of course, but he wasn't so sure he'd be able to lie to them either. Hopefully that was a bridge he'd never have to cross.

Sophia appeared just then with two burgers piled high with toppings. She placed them in front of the guys with an expectant look on her face.

"Another Sophia Special?" Bear asked. He poked at the burger, trying to decipher what all she had put on there.

Sophia smacked his hand away. "No peeking. Just eat."

Derek already had his burger halfway to his mouth. He shot Bear a look that said, *It'll be easier if you just go with it.*

Bear shrugged and took a massive bite, flavor and juice exploding in his mouth and running down his chin. Whatever spice she'd used burned the back of his tongue. Sophia liked to experiment with her food, but she was one of those people who always knew what flavors went with what. Line up five ingredients that, according to nature, should never go in the same dish, and Sophia would have you begging for more.

Maybe it was the distraction of lunch. Maybe it was Derek's rambling appraisal of the burger and Sophia's coy refusal to tell him what was in it. Maybe Bear had just been too relaxed for too long. Or maybe it was because Bear had forgotten what happened when he got too happy.

In any case, he didn't hear the creak of the door as a new customer entered the bar. He didn't notice the man held a gun in his right hand. He didn't even notice as the gunman stood frozen in the doorway as he took in the room before raising his weapon and aiming at their table.

Bear only noticed when the first shot rang out and red blossomed across Derek's chest, his look of euphoria quickly turning to confusion and then pain.

Chapter Two

Sophia's scream is what finally launched Bear into action, but it was already too late. Derek had folded forward, his head coming to rest next to his plate. His eyes wide and lifeless. The burger had dropped from his hand to the floor.

Other people were screaming now and jumping out of the way. Sophia just stood there staring down at her fiancé, another scream threatening to tear from her throat. Bear caught sight of the fire inside her that was only ever a wrong look away, and before he could stop her, Sophia launched herself toward the gunman, a guttural howl of pain and rage escaping her.

The gunman was skinny, like an addict. If Bear got his hands around him, there was no doubt that he'd be able to break the other man in two. But none of that mattered when one person had a gun and the other didn't. The man had wild eyes and was shaking like it'd been too long since his last hit, but Sophia was so close to him now that it would've been impossible to miss.

Both rounds hit dead center when Sophia was just a few feet away. That would stop most people in their tracks. They would've crumpled to the ground right then and there. But Sophia was stronger than most. Bear was certain she was dead on her feet, but her soul must've wanted revenge, too. Instead of collapsing, her body tripped forward and knocked the man off his feet, sending the gun skittering to the side.

That's when Bear decided to move. He found he was already standing, though he didn't remember getting up from the table. One last look at Derek confirmed the man was dead. There'd be time to deal with that later. For now, Bear could only think of one thing: Kill the man who killed his friends.

A loud bang sounded from behind him, causing Bear to whip around, fists at the ready. They wouldn't do much against a gun, but Bear was quicker than he looked. And he had taken more than his fair share of bullets and survived.

But the sound was just the back door banging open as someone pushed their way out of the bar. And as soon as one person found the courage to get up and run, the rest of the customers followed suit. Bear ignored them. The fewer casualties the better. It'd be easier to focus on the gunman if he didn't also have to worry about collateral damage.

When Bear turned back to the other man, however, he was nowhere in sight and the front door of the bar was swinging shut.

Bear sprinted forward, ready to leap over Sophia's body and kill the man who shot her. But a tremor coursing through her body drew him up short. Was she still alive? It seemed impossible, but when he approached her, she turned toward him. A bubble of blood found its way up her throat and down her chin. Her eyes were a mix of despair and terror. Everything had been taken away from her in a matter of seconds. Today was supposed to be like any other day. Instead, it was the end of everything.

The light left her eyes a second later. She went still, her unseeing gaze looking past him. Bear didn't have to turn around to know she had been searching for Derek. Bear checked her pulse just in case, but she was gone.

Instincts kicked in. Bear grabbed the pistol a few feet away and made his way to the door. He counted to three to ready himself, then pushed the door open and scanned the street outside. Deserted. There wasn't a ton of foot traffic on the outskirts of town, but you could always count on seeing one or two lost tourists or an older couple bickering on their way back from the market. The shots must've sent the stragglers scurrying.

The gunman was nowhere in sight. Bear could've gone after him—the island wasn't *that* big—but he looked down at his hands. He didn't remember touching Sophia anywhere other than her neck, but her blood was everywhere. And now his fingerprints were on the handgun.

So Bear fought against the instincts that had initially told him to track down the shooter and kill him, and instead listened to the ones that were telling him to go back inside and wait for the authorities. If he made a spectacle of himself by waving a gun around town, it would only make matters worse. No one knew who he was, but that didn't mean getting arrested wouldn't increase the chance of a red flag being raised. For all he knew, Frank was just waiting for him to screw up so he could send in the dogs.

I t took the authorities ten minutes to get to the scene of the crime. Bear had calmly walked back inside to see if anyone needed any help. The place was deserted, all except for the two bodies. No one else had been injured, it seemed, or if they had, not so bad that they couldn't get away.

Bear wanted to close Sophia's eyes and pick up Derek from his awkward position at the table, but he resisted. He would already have plenty of questions to answer about the blood on his hands and the firearm with his fingerprints. The last thing he wanted to do was make it worse by tampering with the crime scene just because he couldn't stand to see his friends looking this way.

He cursed at himself and felt a flare of anger so hot and deep that it drove him to his knees. He wasn't supposed to be here. Not in this bar. Not in this town. Not on this island. He should've disappeared somewhere remote like Jack had told him to. Get off the grid. Keep your head down. Wait until we know our next move.

They still had to find Thorne and figure out what he was really up to. Their last meeting with the man, when they had tracked him to New York City, had proven that Thorne was better than they had given him credit for. With several snipers bearing down on them, Jack and Bear had only gotten away because Thorne had allowed them to. It hadn't sat well with Jack. God knows neither one of them liked to be outmaneuvered. But it proved that they were in over their heads. They needed to take a step back for a while. Maybe something would come to them.

So Jack went left and Bear went right. He ended up in St. Lucia. It was meant to be a stopover on his way to anywhere else, but one night turned into two and two nights turned into six weeks. He blamed it on the sun. And the beer. And Sophia and Derek's kindness. Bear had felt almost normal for the first time in forever, and that had been his downfall.

No, he thought, looking over at Derek and Sophia's dead bodies. *That had been their downfall. They're the ones who paid the price for your stupidity.*

Bear wasn't sure how long he'd been on his knees like that before both the back and front doors flew open and several officers filed in, guns raised, shouting at him in accented English.

"Drop your weapon! Hands in the air! No sudden movements, or we'll shoot!"

Bear hadn't even realized he was still gripping the pistol. He looked down at it, contemplated his options. But he didn't have any. He let the pistol slip from his fingers and thud to the ground. Then he slowly raised his hands and clasped them behind his head. Strong hands brought one arm down roughly behind him, and then the other. The cold metal of a pair of handcuffs encircled his wrists and brought Bear immediately out of his stupor.

The head officer in front of him, a broad man with dark skin and sharp eyes, lowered his weapon and disappeared back out the door. A few seconds later, he emerged again, this time with an older woman at his side. She was wiry and hunched over, like gravity had years ago started to eat away at her. She was shaking, her eyes never quite looking in the direction of Bear or the dead bodies.

"Is this the man you saw enter with a gun?" the officer asked.

"Yes, yes," the woman replied. Her voice was watery and quiet.

"I need you to say that again, very clearly," the officer asked.

She still didn't look at Bear. "Yes, this is the man with the gun. I saw him."

The officer looked over at one of his deputies and nodded. The other man led the old woman away. Bear was forced to his feet. He was a head and a half taller than the lead officer, but that didn't seem to intimidate him.

"I knew them. They were good people." He stepped closer to Bear, his fists balled tight. *"They were good people."*

Bear swallowed hard. He knew. He had seen it firsthand every day since he'd arrived in St. Lucia. But despite the injustice of it all, and despite the fact that the real killer was still out there, Bear couldn't say anything. Even though he hadn't pulled the trigger, part of him thought he deserved the handcuffs anyway.

Chapter Three

Bear's knees had been forced up to his chest as he was put into the back of the police cruiser. Most cars couldn't accommodate his large frame. It never made road trips any easier. And this was the worst kind of road trip. The officer in charge of transporting him back to the small St. Lucian jail kept glaring at him from the rearview mirror. Bear didn't look away from his gaze. Regardless of his self-imposed guilt, Bear didn't pull the trigger and he wasn't about to act like he did.

The trip was short, but it still felt good to stretch his legs when he finally unfolded himself from the car. He was met by two additional officers and led by the elbows toward the tiny precinct. Bear made sure not to give them a reason to handle him more roughly than they already were. He kept his eyes straight ahead and didn't put up a fight when they shoved him roughly inside a cell with four other men.

The local jail on St. Lucia was small. It had three cells, each filled with an odd mixture of locals and tourists. The stench of alcohol hit Bear as soon as he walked inside. He figured most of his cellmates were there because of the bottle, but a few looked a little sharper, a little more hardened.

Bear turned in his cell after the door closed behind him and stuck his arms through the bars, waiting for one of the officers to remove the cuffs from around his wrists. They were starting to pinch.

A tall, thin officer looked him up and down, the disgust evident on his face. "Murderers don't get the same comforts as everyone else."

Bear bit his tongue. His trademark sarcasm wasn't gonna do him any favors here.

Instead, he turned around and eyed his roommates. There was only one bed, which was occupied by a man Bear's size. His eyes were clear, so Bear figured he was in there for something more than disorderly conduct. He had a scar that ran from the corner of his left eye down to his jaw and over to the tip of his chin, as if someone tried to carve his face like a Thanksgiving turkey.

"You got a problem?" the man asked. He sat up and leaned forward, holding a fist up in front of his face. "I could take care of it for you."

"Take it easy, man. Not looking for trouble."

Bear walked to the other side of the room and leaned up against the wall. He was fairly certain he could take the other man, but Bear had been in the cell for a solid thirty seconds. He wasn't about to rock the boat just yet. Not until he could get a better bead on the rest of his roommates.

There was a man sitting in the corner, sleeping. His mouth hung open, exposing several yellow teeth. Drool ran down the side of his mouth. The strongest stench of liquor was coming from that area, so Bear figured the man wouldn't pose a threat. He'd sleep for the next twelve hours.

A third man stood at the bars, clinging to them like they were his lifeline. He stayed as far away as possible from the man on the cot and kept throwing furtive glances over his shoulder. He was the only other white man in the cell besides Bear. Tourist, maybe.

"There's been some kind of mistake," the man mumbled to himself. He sounded like he was on the edge of tears. "Please. Please let me have my phone call. I need to call my wife. Please."

The officers on the other side of the cell just ignored him, along with the desperate voices that carried over from the two additional cells. Even though this man was dressed in a button-down shirt and a pair of slacks, it looked like he had been in them for at least three or four days.

The last man in the cell was small, at best half Bear's height. He looked frail and weak, but his eyes were sharp. He wore khaki pants and a crumpled polo, and a bowler hat sat atop his head. It looked like he'd blow away in a strong wind, but there was something about him that made Bear look twice. The man looked back. It was a quick, timid glance, but Bear felt like those three seconds were enough for this other guy to read him like a book. But what did he see? And what would he do with that information?

One thing all three of the men had in common, though, was the fact that they weren't in handcuffs. Bear wondered how long the officer would stay posturing like this. He wasn't about to hold his breath.

Bear had been in tight spots before. Most of the time he had Jack at his side. That's because it was usually Jack's fault they were in a tight spot to begin with, but Bear would've given anything to have him there now. Jack would make matters worse—he wasn't exactly good at following the rules—but things always got better after they got worse.

Maybe Bear just needed a catalyst.

Bear pushed off the wall and leaned against the bars next to the tourist. There were four desks in the room outside the cell. There were officers walking back and forth, carrying paperwork or drinking coffee or laughing like there weren't a dozen drunken inmates six feet away from them.

There was one officer still sitting at his desk. It was the tall, thin one that had refused to remove the cuffs. Bear cracked his neck on one side, then the other. There was no telling what would happen here, or how rough the officers got with their prisoners. The precinct was fairly clean and orderly, but it didn't look like the shepherds cared much about their flock.

"Hey," Bear called out. He saw the officer stiffen, but the man didn't turn around. "Hey, Buddy. C'mon. I need to piss."

"There's a drain in the floor," the officer called out over his shoulder.

Bear turned around and, sure enough, there was a small drain on the floor. So maybe that acrid scent wasn't just from the guy in the corner.

"What about lunch? My meal kind of got interrupted."

That hit a nerve. The man stood up so fast, his desk screeched across the floor. In two steps he was in front of Bear. "You want to say that again?"

Bear didn't back down. "I said my meal got interrupted when my friends were killed right in front of me."

The officer put his hand on his gun. Bear didn't miss the movement, but he didn't give the man the satisfaction of looking away from his damning stare.

"You mean when *you* killed Sophia and Derek. For all I care, you can starve."

The man looked Bear up and down one more time and walked away. Bear sighed. Jack was better at getting on people's nerves than he was.

"Do I at least get a phone call?" Bear called out.

The tourist spoke next to him. "Good luck." He laughed, but it was hysterical, like the man was on the edge of a breakdown. "I've been trying for two days. They won't let me call my wife. Or my lawyer." He called out at their captors. "This is unconstitutional! I have rights!"

Bear waved away the comment. "They can say they're understaffed and overrun with delinquents. Lets them get away with anything."

Between one breath and the next, the entire mood of the room shifted. Bear felt more than heard that the large man had gotten up and crossed the room to stand behind him. Moving slowly and deliberately, Bear turned to face him. The other man's face was a mask of anger.

"I don't want any trouble," Bear said. He held up his handcuffed hands, hoping it would make him less threatening.

"Derek gave me a job when no one else would," the man said. "Sophia made sure I had food when my girl kicked me out of the apartment. They were good people."

Bear froze. He had a feeling there wasn't going to be an easy way out of this one. "I know they were good people. They helped me out too."

The man took a step forward. "You killed them."

Bear stood his ground. "I didn't."

"That's not what Jenkins said over there. You calling him a liar?"

"I am," Bear said. "He wasn't there. He didn't see what happened."

The big man looked down at Bear's hands. Bear made the mistake of looking down at them, too. They were still covered in Sophia's blood. When he looked up again, all he saw was a fist coming at his face without any time to do anything but take the hit.

Bear stumbled back and knocked into the tourist, who started calling out for help. Bear scrambled across the room and stood by the smaller man while getting his bearings again. Just when the room came back into focus, there was another fist coming at him. He took another hit, but at least this time he was prepared for it. Didn't stop his nose from gushing blood, though.

The other guy was nearly as big as Bear, but not as fast. The man thought he could get another shot in, but Bear's recovery was damn near instantaneous. He threw up his hands, cursing the cuffs that wouldn't allow him to throw a real punch, and blocked the next two attacks. The man was relentless, but Bear had honed his survival instinct into a weapon to be reckoned with.

Bear clasped his hands together and brought his combined fists down like a hammer. The man's knees buckled but he didn't go down. Instead, he charged. Bear had just enough time to get a leg up and place it in the man's gut, shoving him away and knocking him back into the other two in the cell.

Just as Bear was about to launch himself forward and land a hit that would put the other man down, two pairs of hands grabbed his arms from the other side of the bar and held him back.

"Fuck him up, Javier," one of the men behind him said. It didn't sound like Jenkins, the tall officer.

Javier grinned and wiped the blood from his brow, then stalked toward him. Bear leveraged himself against the bars and the people holding him back and swung his leg up and around. The kick would've landed harder if Bear had been wearing boots instead of sandals, but the result was the same. Bear's foot caught the other man on the side of the head and drove him face first into the wall. The crunch of bone ricocheted around the room before he crumpled to the floor, unconscious.

There was a collective intake of air, like there always was when someone had obviously been seriously injured. Bear didn't pause. He wrenched one arm out of the grip of one of the men behind him, spun around, and pulled one of the second man's hands through the bars. One hand wrapped around the officer's wrist, while the other pushed against the elbow, the cuffs digging into Bear's skin as they were stretched as far as they'd go. Between the jail cell's bar and Bear's hand, the man's arm would give first.

Bear looked up at the officer, whose eyes were wide with terror. Bear leaned forward and whispered to him. "We're both aware that I could snap your arm like a twig and shatter your elbow, right? Nod if you agree." The man nodded frantically. "And we're both aware that I'm choosing not to, right? Nod." The man nodded again, tears in his eyes

Bear let the moment hang for another breath, and then let go. The officer pulled his arm through the opening and backed up against the far wall. He looked like a rookie, and Bear was sure this was the closest he had ever gotten to someone who was being accused of murder.

The second officer was Jenkins. He had pulled his gun and was aiming it at Bear, who raised his hands in front of him and backed up to the bed. He sat down, arms still raised, and waited for someone to do something.

It was the small man who moved first. Slowly, gingerly, he walked over to Javier and placed a pair of fingers against his neck. He looked up at Jenkins. "He's still alive."

Jenkins didn't take his eyes off Bear. "Ramirez. Open the door. Pull Javier out." When the rookie officer stuttered through an excuse, Jenkins cut him off. "Now, Ramirez!"

Bear watched as Ramirez opened the cell with shaking hands and dragged Javier out by his ankles. A smear of blood followed him on the way out. But Bear didn't have any regrets. He wanted a catalyst and he got one.

He put a hand to his nose and wiped away more blood. He just wished it hadn't come to blows. That wasn't going to help his case. But it was worth a try anyway.

"Hey," Bear called out. Jenkins turned around slowly. His gun was still out, but at least it was pointing at the floor now. "Can I get my phone call now?"

Jenkins stared at him for a solid thirty seconds before turning away and dealing with Javier.

"So that's a no, then?" Bear yelled after him.

Chapter Four

After two days, the drunk man in the corner of the cell gained some semblance of consciousness and was allowed to leave. Bear figured he'd be back before long.

The cell felt downright spacious with only Bear and the tiny man sharing the room. When they were finally alone, the other man introduced himself as George. There was no exchanging of stories or sympathies, but there was an unspoken camaraderie there. Bear figured the man hadn't been allowed to sleep on the bed while Javier was king of the cell, so Bear spent that night on the floor.

"Thank you," George said the following morning. His voice was high and quiet, but it had a clarity to it that only came from someone who chose every word with precise calculation. Bear figured that came from years of conditioning when you always had to watch your back. It couldn't have been easy being the smallest guy in the schoolyard. You had to find a way to survive.

"No problem. I've had worse sleeping arrangements."

"American?"

"Yeah."

"You ever been to an American jail?"

"Once or twice."

George bobbed his head up and down, then stared at Bear for a long time, like he was trying to decide what to make of him. "Have you ever been to prison in this part of the world?"

"Once or twice," Bear answered again.

"And how was your experience?"

"As pleasant as can be expected. Prison is prison."

George shook his head and stared up at the ceiling for a moment. "Not here. Not on St. Lucia."

Bear shifted against the wall he was leaning on. He wasn't particularly worried about his current circumstances, but any information he could gather would be worth having. "What do you mean?"

George took several minutes to answer. Bear took a deep breath, held it, and quietly let it go. If George stuck around, he'd have to get used to his information coming a bit slower than usual. Rushing the man would result in the opposite of the desired effect.

"The prison on this island houses only five hundred prisoners or so, but most of them are hardened criminals. Those who are not, who just end up there out of convenience, do not last long. This is not a prison you want to visit, especially if you do not look like you belong."

Bear wasn't sure which part of him didn't belong the most—his size or the color of his skin—but it hardly mattered. He'd stick out in a crowd here, and that usually wasn't a good thing when you were talking about the rec yard.

"I'm guessing the guards don't do much to keep things civil?" Bear asked. He'd been in situations where the guards would turn a blind eye, especially if you caused trouble. He didn't like holding himself back, but Bear recognized when and where a little trouble would help him—and when it would not.

"There are no guards," George answered. "The prison is run by the prisoners. The guards stand on the outside and collect tolls, but they do not go inside unless absolutely necessary. The Sheriff is the oldest prisoner there, and he's the one in charge. Even the guards defer to him. Anyone who gets on the Sheriff's bad side winds up in a very bad position. Or dead."

"What are the chances either one of us will be transferred out of here before we're sent over to the prison?"

"Very low. You've been charged with murder. I am a repeat offender for drug trafficking." George gestured around them. "These cells don't stay empty for long. There is not enough room here to keep anyone other than drunkards and tourists for more than a few days. Everyone else gets transferred and held until the officers have time to deal with the next step."

"And I'm guessing they take their time getting around to that?"

"Depending on the prisoner and his crime? Yes."

Bear leaned his head back against the wall. "Great," he mumbled. "You have any good news for me?"

"I know some people in the prison."

Bear looked at the man. "You been holding out on me, George?"

George shook his head. "I have a few connections, but nothing that will put us in the best part of the prison. One wing is like living at home. You can come and go as you please, eat like a king, enjoy any woman you want. I cannot get us there."

"And the worst part of the prison?"

"You remain in your cell unless you are working for the Sheriff and the upper-class prisoners. It is hard work for no money and very few privileges. But it is better than being dead."

"Can't argue with you there. So, which one can we get?"

"If we're lucky, somewhere in the middle."

Bear scratched at his chin. "Which means what, exactly?"

"Some freedom, with nights spent in our cells. No visitors. Light work. But we must still be careful. Prisoners are transferred from one wing to the other depending on their behavior. We can move up, but we can also move down."

"Fair enough." Bear cut a glance at the small man and sized him up. He was proving useful, but there was always a catch in these types of situations. "What do you want in return?"

George paused again, this time for several minutes. Bear started to meditate so his blood pressure wouldn't spike. He was just starting to really relax when George spoke again.

"Protection."

"Figured as much. You got any enemies in there I need to know about?"

"Everyone is an enemy," George said, "until they prove they are a friend."

Bear couldn't argue with that.

The following day, Bear felt like he finally got his first break. He was dozing on the bed, having switched off with George the night before, when someone banged on the bars. Bear was awake immediately, but he kept his eyes closed. He was suddenly much less worried about pissing off these guards and saving up all his good behavior for when he was undoubtedly transferred.

"Logan," the voice said. It sounded like Jenkins. "Get up. You get one phone call."

Bear was out of bed and at the cell door in less than three seconds. He didn't care about looking desperate. If he could contact someone, he had no doubt all of this would be over in no time. He wouldn't be transferred to prison and he could be well on his way to some other island in paradise. Only this time he wouldn't befriend the locals. Less of a chance of being charged with murder that way.

Hell, maybe he could even set George up with a better situation.

Jenkins opened the door, and two other officers escorted Bear to a pay phone on the far wall, then took a step back and crossed their arms over their chests at the same time, watching him.

Bear laughed. "You practice that in the mirror?"

They didn't answer. Bear shrugged and turned around. Now was the moment of truth. Who should he call?

Jack was his first instinct. He was the only person he trusted without a shred of doubt. But he was also off the grid. Pulling him out of hiding could put both of them in a spotlight neither one of them wanted to be in at the moment. The deal was to lay low for as long as possible. Bear kind of screwed the pooch on that one.

He could also call Frank. He didn't trust the man as far as he could throw him, but Frank needed Bear. He'd come through, even if it would be reluctantly. But Bear still held a grudge against Frank. He was a manipulative bastard, and Bear didn't like the idea of owing Frank any favors.

There were a few other people Bear could call, people he trusted, but no one with the means or pull that either Jack or Frank had.

"You've only got two more minutes," one of the officers said. "I suggest you make use of them. You won't get any more."

Bear's grip on the receiver tightened. He didn't know he was on a time limit, but he wasn't going to waste time arguing with the two punks behind him.

Instead, Bear dialed the one person he could trust no matter the circumstances. Once he got hold of him, Jack could reach out to Frank if it became necessary. But just having someone know where he was would help. Someone who would be on his side.

Bear dialed the number from memory. It was a line that Jack kept open only for Bear, for when things were desperate. He hated to admit it, but things were desperate now. Bear had no doubt he could survive the prison George had described to him for a few days, even a few weeks. But longer than that? Bear always attracted the wrong kind of attention, and he didn't think this was the kind of place he wanted to take chances in.

The line rang once, twice, three times. And then four. It kept ringing. Bear got to double digits and continued to count. His heart started to beat faster. Some sort of voicemail should've picked up by now. If he could at least leave a message, he'd know Jack would get it eventually.

The receiver was ripped out of his hand and placed back on the hook. Bear's head snapped around. He was face to face with Jenkins.

"Time's up."

"He didn't answer," Bear sputtered. He was so sure Jack would pick up. He was so sure calling Jack was the right move. "I need to try again."

"You only get one phone call," Jenkins said.

Bear began to resist. Even with three officers on him, they couldn't move him more than a foot back toward his cell. "I need to try again."

Jenkins let go. Bear thought he was going to give him another shot at calling Jack, but when he turned around, all Bear saw was a police baton coming for his temple and then everything went black.

Chapter Five

B ear had a single day to recover from the hit to his head, and then he and George were dressed in orange jumpsuits, shackled together, and placed in a small bus with a handful of other prisoners. The trip was short and bumpy, and Bear was sweating through his clothes in a matter of minutes. George looked more resigned than afraid, but somehow that didn't comfort Bear.

He had a bad feeling about this place, and all of it had to do with the fact that he hadn't been able to get in touch with Jack. It was one thing to wait things out while Jack worked on the problem at hand. But Jack didn't even know there was a problem. He was probably on some beach drinking Bahama Mamas just because he knew Bear wouldn't be able to laugh at him.

Bear definitely wasn't laughing.

No one knew where he was. That meant the only way he'd be leaving this prison was if he was proven innocent or he escaped. He had more faith in the idea of escaping than getting off the hook, but if what George had said was true, this place was locked down unless you had money or something as valuable to offer.

At the moment, Bear had nothing more than his fists and his wits. Usually that was more than enough to get out of any scrape, but he wasn't so sure this time. Bear looked over at George. The tiny man was his greatest asset. He still didn't know what kind of people George knew inside the prison, but it was worth keeping the guy safe. He might end up being his only ticket out of there.

But how long would that be? Months? Years? Bear liked to think Jack would be able to track him down eventually when Bear didn't answer any of his phone calls, but they had both agreed to go off the grid. That meant taking every precaution not to be found, even by each other.

Bear's thoughts were cut short when the bus screeched to a stop. The driver opened the door and a broad man in an officer's uniform and hat stepped onboard. The bus tipped a little and then righted itself once he made it to the center aisle. Bear figured the man weighed about as much as he did. But he also had to remind himself that he wouldn't be dealing with this guy, or any other officer at the prison. These were just border control. The real threats were inside.

"My name is Officer Davis. For the few of you who don't know who I am—" he looked directly at Bear when he said this "—you'll soon find out that nothing and no one comes into or out of this prison without my knowledge. You'll find that I can be very forgiving if you don't cause any trouble. So just keep that in mind."

Bear could read between the lines. Not causing trouble was synonymous with paying him off. Bear had a stash of money hidden away, but he wasn't sure if he could get to it from inside the prison. Right now, his currency was George's knowledge and connections. That would have to be enough.

Davis looked out over his prisoners, once again landing on

Bear a little longer than the rest. Then he turned around and got off the bus, calling over his shoulder, "File out!"

Bear stood and followed George off the bus. It was obvious the trees had been cleared out to give the officers a line of sight around the prison. It resulted in direct sunlight that beat down on them as they stood outside a concrete wall that must've been at least twelve feet tall and covered in barbed wire. There would be no climbing over it without being caught. Bear would have to either tunnel underneath or walk out through the front door.

"Welcome back, Charles," Davis said, turning to one of the prisoners. "Block 4, huh? Movin' up."

A man stepped forward. His hair was buzzed short and his head was covered in tattoos, as was his neck and arms. Bear figured the rest of him was too. He was tall, but lean. There was plenty of muscle there, even if he didn't have the same bulk as Bear. He looked fast, too. The way he moved and held himself, Bear figured he'd been in and out of this place plenty of times for Davis to remember his name.

"That's right," Charles said. "Lap of luxury."

"Better enjoy it while you can," Davis said, uncuffing the man. "Heard your stay might not be that long this time."

Charles laughed. "We'll see about that."

George shuffled closer to Bear, who had to lean down to hear him.

"Living on Block 4 is basically like living on the outside, but in many cases, a felon can make a lot more money here than anywhere else in the Caribbean."

"Prison is still prison," Bear said. "You're still confined by four walls."

George shrugged. "You could say the same thing about a house. Some walls are more profitable than others."

Davis let Charles walk through the front gate on his own. He greeted two other guards on his way in, and Bear heard the cheers of several inmates upon Charles' return. It was starting to dawn on Bear how important it was going to be that he knew anyone at all inside the prison, let alone someone who was potentially connected.

"Block 3," Davis called out.

Three prisoners stepped forward. Davis checked their names against a list and waved them on. The three men stayed close to each other as they walked through the gate, which told Bear they had either come to an agreement on the ride over to stick together, or they had formed an alliance the last time they were in prison together.

"Block 2," Davis called out.

George stepped forward, along with two others. Bear hesitated, and then joined them. There was one man left. He was shaking, with tears in his eyes. He wouldn't last the night. George hadn't told him what Block 1 was like, but being at the bottom rung in any prison wasn't a good position to be in, let alone at a place like this.

"Stay close to me," George whispered.

George let the two other men go before him. Once they were escorted through the door, Davis looked back at the tiny man, up at Bear, and then back down at George.

"Nice to see you again, George."

George's voice sounded stronger and harder when he spoke. "You too, Officer Davis. How're the kids?"

"Little shits," Davis said. "But good as can be expected." He paused, glancing at Bear again. "You know he's not on the list for Block 2."

"Malik is good for it. You know he is."

"Gonna cost you extra."

"Of course. We'll pay."

Davis chuckled, wrote a note down on the clipboard, and

uncuffed both of them. "I hope he's worth it, George. I expect payment by the end of the night."

"You'll have it before dinner's over."

Davis shook his head. "I like you, George. Don't make promises you can't keep. I'd hate to put you on my shit list."

George just nodded and began the trek toward the gate.

Bear hurried to catch up. "Why do I have a feeling that was all bullshit?"

George smiled, but kept his eyes steady on the gate in front of them. "My cousin, Malik, runs Block 2. He paid ahead to get me into his wing. He won't be happy to have to pay for you, too. You'll have to work it off."

"And how do I know he won't just kill me on the spot? Then he won't have to pay anything." Bear already felt the tension entering his shoulders. His body was getting ready for a fight.

George waved away the comment. "Malik is a businessman. He'll find a use for you."

"Why doesn't that make me feel any better?"

"Because you are a smart man, Riley Logan."

Chapter Six

They had to walk through Block 1 to get to Block 2. It was more like a shanty town than a prison. There were lean-tos and tents instead of cells. Most of the inmates here looked malnourished and sleep-deprived.

"These are the prisoners who cannot afford to buy or rent a cell in Block 2 or higher," George explained. "They work for the other prisoners, doing the jobs no one else wants to do. Most of them will never leave Block 1. They must pay tolls to go from one Block to another in order to work, and then protection on top of that. They will either be released as a Block 1 prisoner or die here."

"You have to buy your cell?" Bear asked. The stench around him turned his stomach, but he didn't let it show on his face.

George nodded. "You must pay for everything here. If you can afford it, you'll live like a king. If you can't, you'll die like a slave."

They crossed the yard, being careful not to trample anyone's living space. They may have been Block 2 prisoners, but messing with a man's living quarters, however shitty, meant fists would fly regardless of station.

When they made it to the door on the other side, another guard waited for them. This wasn't an officer, but another prisoner. He had his own clipboard, and despite only guarding the door between Blocks 1 and 2, he took his job seriously.

"Name?"

"George Baptiste."

The man looked through his list, then tapped it with his pencil. "You're clear. Who's your friend?"

"Riley Logan," George said. He cleared his throat. "He's not on the list."

The man looked up sharply. "Then he can't go through."

"My cousin is Malik King. He will vouch for him."

The man threw back his head and laughed. Bear only counted six or seven teeth. "Do you know how many men claim Mailk is their cousin, their uncle, their brother? You can go through. He cannot."

George turned back to Bear with sympathetic eyes. "I will talk to Malik and get you through by the end of the night."

"And you're sure you can convince your cousin to sponsor me?" Bear asked. George had gotten him this far, but prison politics were a dangerous game to play. Blood meant a lot in here, but it wouldn't stop one brother from killing the other if he thought it would keep him at the top of the food chain.

"Trust me," George said, slipping through the opening in the door to Block 2. "Trust me."

George held true to his word.

Bear had set himself up against a wall close to the door where no one would bother him. Some of the prisoners coming and going from Block 2 would give him a once-over, but no one approached. He had a feeling that wouldn't last the night, especially if he needed to find a spot to sleep in, but luckily George came through before that presented itself as a necessity.

The door slid open and George shuffled across the threshold, followed by a man who was only a couple heads taller, but much broader. His skin was darker, but his eyes were brighter, like bronze bullets set into his head. He wore his hair in dreadlocks that came to his shoulders, and instead of a prisoner jumpsuit, he wore jeans and a T-shirt. Bear figured this, more than anything else, was a sign of his stature within the prison.

"Malik, this is Riley Logan," George said.

"Bear." He stuck his hand out.

Malik hesitated for a moment, looking Bear up and down, before grasping his hand and giving it a hard shake.

"My cousin here tells me you've been looking out for him."

"That's right."

"He wants me to pay for you to cross over into Block 2 and split a cell with him."

Bear didn't say anything.

"Nothing in here is free." Malik gestured around him. "I'm where I am today because I paid my dues. I don't give handouts."

"Not looking for one," Bear said.

"Then what are you looking for?"

"A business arrangement."

Malik chuckled and cast a glance over his shoulder to the guard at the door, who laughed on cue. But Bear didn't miss the way Malik's eyes lit up. "What kind of arrangement?"

"If you put me in Block 2 with George, I'll keep an eye out for him, just like I have been."

"I've got plenty of other people who are willing to do the same." Malik crossed his arms over his chest. "Why should I choose you instead of them?"

"I'm cheaper," Bear said. "And more trustworthy."

Malik laughed even louder this time. "More trustworthy?"

Bear shrugged. It was a risk, but one worth taking this early in the game. "I've got no interest in politics. I'm counting on the fact that I won't be here for long. I want to repay my debt to George for getting me this far. I'm willing to put in the work, and I'm not interested in trying to climb the ladder and unseat the person at the top."

Malik dropped a heavy hand on Bear's shoulder. He did his best not to tense up.

"You couldn't unseat me if you tried, friend," Malik said. "But I like the idea of having someone who's willing to put in the work for next to no glory. I applaud your optimism for thinking you won't be here for long. I have no problem taking advantage of that until reality sets in."

Malik turned toward the guard and nodded his head. There was no hesitation this time. Malik's word was law, and the guard wasn't about to break the rules. He stepped aside and allowed all three men to pass.

The differences between Block 1 and Block 2 were immediately apparent. The stench nearly cut off from one sector to the other, and there were actual cells here. Unlike other prisons, most of the cell doors were open, with the inmates walking back and forth between each other's rooms or down along the corridor and around the corner.

"George tells me you've never been to a prison like our humble Rehabilitation Center," Malik said. "What do you think so far?"

"I think rehabilitation center is an interesting choice of words," Bear said, walking past a pair of men sharpening a pair of rusty knives.

Malik threw his head back and laughed again. He did everything loudly. You couldn't ignore him if you tried, but no one was that stupid. He looked every prisoner in the eye as he passed, like it was a challenge.

Will you try to kill me today?

What about you?

But no one made an attempt. Everyone either said hello or nodded their head by way of greeting. Show respect and you get respect. It was a game Bear knew well. It's a lesson the military taught him a long time ago.

"True, true," Malik said. "But in a way, it's still true. The prison is rehabilitating us, but instead of making us better citizens, it's making us better criminals."

Malik found this concept hilarious. Bear looked down to George, but the smaller man didn't share his cousin's enthusiasm. It made Bear wonder, not for the first time, why Malik was so interested in keeping his cousin safe to begin with. Family only went so far. George had to be useful, too.

The group stopped at the end of the hallway, and Bear saw that the corridor turned and continued on. The cells here looked bigger and cleaner. They had more decorations, more personal touches. There were even guards posted outside some of them.

Malik turned and looked at Bear before moving on. "But tell me. What do you really think of this place?"

It felt like a test. Malik obviously had pride in what he did on Block 2. If Bear told him it was a shithole, he'd get offended. But if he sucked up too much, it would come across as disingenuous. Bear couldn't afford either outcome that resulted from those reactions.

"You obviously run a tight ship and have the respect of the other inmates. It's a step up from Block 1. But prison is still prison, man."

Malik was silent for a moment. Bear could feel him digesting what he'd said, looking for insults inside of compliments. Finally, he nodded his head and dropped another heavy hand on his shoulder. "That it is, that it is. Let me show you to your cell. Then we can talk business arrangements."

Chapter Seven

There were eight different corridors in Block 2, and it became immediately obvious to Bear that the further he got away from the Block 1 door, the nicer the cells became. Malik made sure to give them the full tour, which consisted of walking them by his cell right by the Block 3 door. It looked like they had knocked down the walls between several cells in order to make one big one that looked to be three times larger than anyone else's. There was a full bed, actual furniture, and two guards standing outside to make sure no one messed with his stuff.

The cell Bear would share with George was near the middle of the block. It was comfortable enough for the two of them, with a bunk bed and a small dresser. It was wicker and looked like it would fall apart if one of them sneezed too loudly, but in a place like this, it was an obvious sign of money. Or power.

Once again Bear had to wonder what it was that made George so special. Malik clearly had respect for his cousin for one reason or another, but Bear couldn't figure out why. Maybe it was because he was a good contact to have on the outside, but now that he was in here, what could George provide to make sure Malik kept him around?

"I got George a job on Block 3 in the kitchens. It's not great work, but it pays well enough and no one will bother him there. Plus, I like the idea of having eyes and ears in there."

Was that what George was good at? He was unassuming enough. Bear wondered if Malik hid the fact that they were related so no one would bother him. Or think he was a spy.

"And what will I be doing?" Bear asked.

"The kitchens always need more hands, so you'll have a job there, too."

"What will I really be doing?"

Malik clapped and looked over at George, his eyebrows raised. "I'm proud of you, cousin. You found a smart one!" He laughed and turned back to Bear. "Your real job is making sure George stays safe."

Bear hedged his bets. "This isn't just about protecting your own, is it?"

Malik rubbed at his chin. "Blood is important. Blood connects people. Our mothers were sisters. My Aunt Bea took care of me when my mom disappeared for weeks at a time. I owe it to her to take care of him."

"But that's not the only reason."

Malik took his time responding this time. "George is useful in other ways. That big brain of his has come in handy. He hears a lot and he remembers everything. He's good with numbers. He's helped me to get where I am today, so he gets special treatment."

Not special enough, Bear thought, looking around at their Spartan room. But he was smart enough not to say anything.

Instead, he walked inside the cell and tested the bottom mattress. It was thin. He'd be sore the next morning, but not as sore as if he'd slept on the ground.

"You expect trouble?" Bear asked.

"Always," Malik said. "Not many people know he's my inside man, but secrets don't stay secret long here. We'll have to pull you guys eventually. Nothing good lasts forever."

It was Bear's turn to laugh, but there wasn't as much glee in it. "Don't I know it."

Malik weighed his words before he spoke next. "What's your background?"

Bear played dumb. "American."

"Don't do that." Any humor on Malik's face disappeared in an instant. "I'm not a good person to test boundaries with. Answer the question."

"Military. Cut ties a while back. Started to freelance. Got into some shit. That's why I'm here."

The humor returned to Malik's face. "Big, smart, and used to following orders? I'm liking you more and more, Bear."

"So what's next?" Bear asked. He wasn't interested in letting the interrogation go on longer than necessary.

"Sleep," Malik said, backing out of the room. "Tomorrow is the first day of your new life."

Bear could tell that Malik ran a tight ship as soon as he entered Block 2, but even he was impressed by the way the man controlled the inmates under his supervision. The old hats who had worked their way up the ladder made sure the rookies stayed in line. There was a clear divide among the inmates. Those who had power and those who did not. Those who were in the know and those who were not.

George didn't have power, per se, but power was on his side. Those who knew it left him alone. Those who didn't left him alone too, but that was likely because of Bear's presence. Plus they had seen Malik giving them a personal tour. You didn't have to be that smart to put two and two together.

There was a timekeeper on the block, and as soon as the sun was above the horizon, he went from corridor to corridor waking everyone up. Bear was already awake. He hadn't slept much. He doubted it was the bed—he could sleep just about anywhere—so it was more likely the new surroundings. The bars on his cell may have had a door, but it wasn't locked. The inmates had to be able to come and go, after all.

"That's Hassan," George said. He had taken the top bunk the night before. "He's Malik's right hand man. Everything goes through him first. He has as many spies as Malik."

Bear rubbed the sleep off his face. "And Malik trusts him?"

"As much as you can trust someone in here." George jumped down from his bed and landed lightly on his feet. "They've both got nukes, so to speak. What's that called? They could use them on each other, but then they'll probably both die."

"Mutually assured destruction."

"Yes." George did some light stretching while he talked. "Instead, they work together. That way—"

"They've got twice as many nukes," Bear finished.

George nodded his head. "Come on. We don't want to be late on our first day."

Bear let George take the lead. Most everyone was up and out of their cells, but there were a few looking out forlornly from behind their bars. Bear figured some of them were being punished for one reason or another and were being locked in. This was confirmed when Hassan passed them a second time, a ring of keys jingling loudly from his hip.

Most of the inmates lined up along the wall and started shuffling along toward the door to Block 3. Bear avoided eye contact, but he still sized up every man around him. Most of them were exactly the kind of men you'd expect to see in prison: tall, broad, angry, and covered in tattoos. There weren't a lot of weaker looking men in here. That made George an anomaly. Which also made him a target. Bear figured he'd have his work cut out for him trying to keep his new friend safe.

Malik was waiting at the door to Block 3, watching as his men passed from one side to the other. George stepped up to give the guard his name while Malik halted the line in order to talk to Bear.

"Your fees for crossing from Block 1 to Block 2 have been paid. I've also sponsored your cell and your daily passage into Block 3 for your work. Your earnings from your job will be passed to me when you get paid at the end of every week. You've got some catching up to do, Bear."

"I'm not worried about it."

Malik grinned, no doubt remembering Bear's confidence that he wouldn't be here for long. "I just want you to know that we're only square when your debt has been paid, regardless of whether you're on this side of the wall or not. Officer Davis is a good friend of mine. We have a very promising business arrangement. I might not be able to find you once you leave here, but he most certainly can."

Bear got the threat loud and clear. He'd have to deal with that later. For now, he had to focus on getting through the day. Then he could worry about how he was going to escape this hellhole.

Malik waved him on and the line was allowed to start moving again. Bear gave his name to the guard and passed through into Block 3, where George was waiting for him. It was immediately obvious how much better off the prisoners of Block 3 were than those from Block 2.

The main corridor was wider, and each cell was bigger than Bear's. Everyone's room was decked out with more furniture and pictures and personal items, and everyone had a guard for their cell. In fact, several of the prisoners from Block 2 took up residence outside of one cell or another as soon as they passed

45

through the door. This was their 9–5 while their bosses left their rooms and did whatever they pleased.

The inmates who were to work in the kitchens were led down the hallway and out into a courtyard. Block 2 didn't even have a recreation area. If you wanted fresh air or to use the free weights, you had to pay to pass through the door and then again to stay in the yard. Everything had its price in here.

The courtyard was twice as big as the open area in Block 1, with several points of ingress and egress. Nearly everyone here was dressed like Malik, in casual clothes. It was immediately obvious that Bear and the others were merely visitors who were lucky enough to be able to cross over.

Bear could feel the stares of the Block 3 inmates as they walked by, but he didn't bother looking back. Better not to cause any trouble on the first day, and one look in the wrong direction could send the whole rec yard into a frenzy. As much as he hated doing it, Bear kept his head down and stuck close to George.

When they made it to the kitchens, everyone split off to do the jobs they'd been doing for several years. The man who had led them from one end of the block to the other turned to George, Bear, and one other newcomer. He was a large man, covered in sweat, with three gold teeth and a scar running across his neck. His voice sounded like there was gravel caught in his throat.

"You." He pointed to the other man. "Cleaning duty."

The man didn't look happy, but he didn't bother saying anything. Washing dishes and making sure surfaces stayed clean was one of the most thankless jobs in a kitchen, and it was ten times worse in prison.

The big man turned to them next. "You George? And Bear?"

"That's right," Bear answered.

"Prep duty," he said, then turned on his heel and walked away.

George looked up at Bear and shrugged, then made his way forward to figure out what they were supposed to do next. Bear figured this was another favor from Malik. Bear was big enough to do the heavy lifting in the kitchen, but instead he was allowed to stay with George in the prep station. There was no way someone hadn't been paid under the table to pull that one off.

For the first time, Bear allowed himself to worry that he wouldn't be able to pay his debts to Malik and what that would mean for his chances of getting out of this place.

Chapter Eight

Any prison, even the St. Lucian Rehabilitation Center, is good at teaching you one thing: routine.

Every day, Bear would wake up at the same time, shuffle along in the same line, pass through the same door, cross the same courtyard, and work in the same kitchen. He'd chop vegetables and slice meat. He'd unwrap freeze-dried concoctions that looked no better than the MREs he'd eaten while serving, and pass them on to the next person to put out for the inmates who couldn't afford a decent meal.

He was constantly surrounded by putrid and repugnant odors, whether it be from the food he was handling or the men he had to work with. In a single day he learned how to distinguish Block 1 inmates from Block 2 inmates from Block 3 inmates based solely on body odor alone. His appetite decreased with every passing hour, but he forced himself to swallow the cheapest items on the menu. He couldn't afford to be in any more debt, but he had to make sure he kept his strength up.

And when his last meal was consumed, he tidied up his work

space and made the trek backwards through the same courtyard, the same door, and the same line. He and George would both collapse into their beds, too tired from standing on their feet all day to entertain a game of cards from one of the few men on Block 2 who decided to pay them any mind.

They rarely saw Malik, other than when they were passing from one block to the other. From what Bear could gather, his job was collecting debts. He mainly stayed within Block 2, but he'd sometimes venture into Block 3 or make a trip into Block 1. It was always with a small guard and it was always for hours at a time. Bear figured he was either making deals or breaking legs. He came back with bloody fists more often than not.

Bear got paid once a week. It was a measly sum on the outside, but it actually went quite far within the prison walls. He only kept enough to pay for his meals every day. The rest went straight to Malik. At first Malik tried to refuse the money, telling Bear to spend it on some quality perks—booze, cigarettes, women—but Bear refused. He wasn't interested in extending his stay, and Malik surprisingly didn't push. It must've been nice to meet a convict who didn't try to con him out of a deal.

George kept his deal with Malik a secret. Bear saw the two exchange money on several occasions, but he also saw Malik put some coins back in his cousin's hand frequently. Whether it was for additional protection, for luxuries, or for something else, Bear never knew, and George never brought it up. Every once in a while, however, he'd come back from the kitchen with a treat— fresh fruit or a rare dessert. He always offered some to Bear. Bear always refused. He was starting to get a soft spot for the man, and he liked seeing him happy.

Two weeks had passed within the prison walls and Bear felt like he was no closer to getting out. He had never really had hope that Jack would come for him, and if his friend did figure out where he was, it wouldn't be for several more months, if not longer. And Bear didn't quite trust Malik enough to call on him for another favor, especially one as big as this.

Bear's plan was simple. He'd keep his head down and continue to work off his debt to Malik. Once he was square, he'd ask the man for a trade. He'd do him a favor in exchange for a way out. Bear knew the favor would have to be a big one, like taking out a major player in Block 3. He was no stranger to violence or killing, but the idea still didn't sit well with him. Every inmate was tied to one another on some level, and the chances of killing someone and not bringing half the prison down on top of him in the process was slim to none.

But he refused to die in here.

The sound of Hassan banging on his bars was enough to bring him out of his thoughts and onto his feet. Another day, another few cents in his pocket. The worst thing about prison wasn't the food or the other prisoners or even the walls you were surrounded by. It was your own mind. Once you start to give up, there's no turning back.

Constant movement was the only solution. Keeping his head down and his feet shuffling forward was all Bear could do to get through the day without losing himself.

And that was the problem. Keeping his head down was the right move to keep his head where it needed to be, but it also meant he didn't see the attack when two prisoners charged straight for George as soon as they got halfway across Block 3's rec yard.

One minute George was walking in front of him, and the next his feet were off the ground and he was flying toward one of the walls. He hit it with a sickening crunch, then crumpled to the floor and didn't move.

Bear looked up in time to see the fist of a bald-headed man flying toward his face. He dodged, but not quickly enough. The other man's knuckles caught him on the corner of his jaw. It wasn't enough to do any real damage, but it was enough to rattle his brain a bit.

Before he could recover, though, another fist hit him in the stomach. This one was from a different man, someone with significantly more hair than the first guy but significantly less body mass. Still, he was quick on his feet. He moved like a boxer, darting in with a *jab, jab, jab*, and then darting out again before Bear could lay a hand on him.

Bear managed to dodge the bigger man's second right hook, using the momentum to send the other guy to the ground. He looked behind him, at George, where there was a third man, much shorter and thinner than the other two, kicking him in the ribs.

Instinct kicked in. Bear felt more than saw the boxer moving in for his next assault, and instead of trying to get out of the way, he moved forward and took the three blows to the gut, tightening his muscles as best he could so the wind wouldn't be knocked out of him. This surprised the other man just long enough for Bear to throw a fist at the man's head and lay him out. He wouldn't be getting up any time soon.

George was tough for his size, but the thin man was relentless. His constant barrage of kicks was starting to take their toll on George, despite the fact that he had curled himself up into a ball. There was blood on the ground, and even from several feet away Bear could hear George's quiet whimpering. He wouldn't be able to last much longer.

For a fleeting moment, Bear wondered where the guards were. Other inmates were starting to gather now. Some were already placing bets on the fight. Others were looking hungry enough to move in themselves and try to get a piece of the action. If Bear could just last long enough for the guards to come in and stop the fight, both he and George could walk away from this relatively unharmed.

But then Bear remembered that there were no guards, only inmates. And he was on Block 3, well away from the safety Malik provided. He was in another man's territory, and this fight was more than likely orchestrated. Why else would three inmates simultaneously attack him and George? Malik had warned them he had enemies.

The bigger man was getting to his knees now, anger in his eyes at being forced to the ground. Bear took the few seconds he had to sprint to George's side and rip the thin man away from him. He flung him nearly as far as the bigger man had flung George, though there was no sickening crunch this time. Instead, the thin man rolled to a stop, sprung to his feet, and waited for another opportunity to move in. He wasn't a fighter, just an opportunist.

The bald-headed man was a fighter, though. He matched Bear in size, but his form was sloppy. He used brute strength and intimidation to win his fights. Bear used his brain. When the big man charged him one more time, Bear once again used his momentum against him. He stepped to the side and pushed the other man past him, forcing him to connect, head first, with the wall. This time there was a sickening crunch.

Bear made sure the bald-headed man stayed down before looking up at the crowd in front of him. Several new figures moved forward. Bear had the stamina to continue the fight, and with his back to the wall, he could hold out against several more opponents.

But he couldn't hold out against all of them. If they wanted to, the entirety of Block 3 could attack at once, and that would be the end of both George and Bear altogether.

It wasn't in his nature to give in, though, so Bear raised his fists and prepared for the next fight. That's when a voice rang out.

"That's enough."

Bear couldn't tell where it had come from. Somewhere in the back, off to the right, but he couldn't spot the person. The voice echoed across the courtyard, but it was quiet somehow. Soft. There was a lot of power in that voice, a lot of control. It was like sitting behind the wheel of a Ferrari and knowing when you needed to back off to take a turn and when you could really open it up on a straightaway.

The crowd parted and a man stepped to the front. He had bronze skin and short, dark hair. He looked Native American and stood out in the prison yard as much as Bear did because of it. He dressed like he was getting ready for an interview, with checkered button-down shirt and slacks. Actual dress pants. Bear couldn't believe his eyes.

The man stopped beside the boxer, who was just now able to sit up, though he was still blinking the stars from his eyes. The man in the button-down shirt looked at him, disappointed. "I think Malik will get the message, won't he? Go take George back to his block. He's in no shape to work today."

Bear widened his stance in front of George, who was still cowering and whimpering on the ground. He wasn't about to let him out of his sight.

"I wouldn't do that if I were you," the man in the button-down said. His voice was refined. "We have no intention of killing George. Just sending a little message to his cousin, who seems to have gotten too big for his station."

"I'll take him back myself," Bear said.

"No," the man said. "You're gonna follow me. I want to have a little chat with you, Bear."

Bear recovered fairly quickly from the momentary shock that this man knew his name. "And if I refuse?"

"Then you both die."

Chapter Nine

Bear had no choice but to trust that the man in the button-down shirt wasn't bluffing, but he waited until George was carried across the courtyard and out of sight before he moved. Then he merged into the crowd, only looking back once to see the bald-headed man being dragged in the opposite direction, probably to the infirmary.

"My name is Kafka," the man in the button-down shirt said. "I'd like you to have lunch with me."

Bear didn't bother being polite. He had too much pent-up energy. "It's not like you're giving me much choice."

"I gave you a choice," Kafka said, his voice forever measured. "You're just smart enough to make the right one."

"Why do you want me to have lunch with you?" Bear didn't feel like playing games today, but he had quickly learned over the past couple weeks that it didn't much matter what he wanted.

"You impressed me out there today." Kafka nodded at a guard and the door to one of the Block 3 wings opened for both of them. With one checkered arm extending out in front of him, Kafka politely motioned for Bear to go first. "You performed much better than I thought you would."

Bear walked through the door, body ready for an attack. Kafka must have noticed because he laughed.

"No more harm will come to you, Bear. You passed my test."

"Yeah? What's my prize?"

Kafka waved a finger, a slight admonition for Bear's attitude. "Your life, for one. Lunch, for another. And perhaps a business arrangement, if you're interested."

"I'm not," Bear said, stopping in the middle of the hallway. There were only a few inmates in here, since most of them were outside in the courtyard, but he still felt trapped. He was in the lion's den now. "I've got enough business arrangements to last me a lifetime."

"Yes, you've currently got something worked out with Malik on Block 2, isn't that right?"

Bear didn't bother answering. Kafka already knew it was true.

"I can propose something better."

"And why would you do that?"

Kafka didn't answer right away. Instead, they continued to walk down the stark white hallway toward what could only be his cell. It was more like a small apartment. It took up half the wing and had real walls and a door. There were no bars here. You could almost forget you were a prisoner.

Again, Bear was motioned through the door first. He stepped over the threshold, expecting to find a few of Kafka's men waiting for them. Instead, they were alone. Bear looked back over his shoulder. Kafka was lean but didn't strike him as much of a fighter. The thought must've shown on Bear's face.

"One shout is all it will take to send half the wing running in here," Kafka said.

Bear shrugged. There was no point in denying it. "I could do some serious damage by then."

"True." Kafka bobbed his head up and down like a bird. His neck was unnaturally long. "But you'd be dead and I'd be out of an investment. We'd both lose, but you more than me. Is that what you want?"

Bear took a seat on one of the wooden chairs. The fact that it had a cushion was a sign of this man's power. Bear was hoping the fact that he was making himself at home without invitation would annoy Kafka, but it made him smile. Bear prodded instead. "An investment?"

"I allowed you and George Baptiste to take up in the kitchens. I made sure you had decent work. I paid my men to leave you alone for two weeks."

"Malik got us those jobs."

"Nothing happens without my knowledge or my permission." Kafka took a seat opposite Bear and crossed one leg over the other. The movement was almost dainty. "Malik was able to get you those jobs because I allowed it."

Bear was getting tired of the pleasantries. "So you pull all the strings on Block 3, do you?"

"No, no, no," Kafka said, a grin on his face. "I run one wing for our block leader. I'm privileged, of course, but by no means am I in charge."

"But you'd like to be," Bear said.

"Perhaps one day."

Bear stood up suddenly. Kafka didn't even flinch. Somehow that annoyed Bear even more. "Unless you're gonna get to the point, pal, I'm leaving."

"Patience, Bear," Kafka said. He put his hands up in surrender. "We can at least eat first, right? No charge, I promise."

Bear's stomach betrayed him and growled loudly enough for Kafka to hear. The other man laughed, reached over, and rang a little bell that was sitting on his wooden dresser.

Thirty seconds passed and then two men came into the room,

each carrying a tray of food. Real food. Not the soup and gruel Bear usually had to eat. There were fruits and vegetables. Sandwiches. Even a cheese platter.

Bear's stomach growled again as the men placed the trays on the table between them and left, but he didn't reach for the food. Instead, he turned to Kafka. "In here, everything has a price."

With delicate fingers, Kafka plucked a sandwich from the middle of the tray. "My only price is for you to sit, enjoy the food, and listen to what I have to say. Nothing more. I promise."

As much as Kafka professed that Bear had a choice, he knew better. Not only did Bear doubt he'd be able to leave the wing without at least entertaining this proposition, but he'd have to answer to Malik when he returned to Block 2. If everything was going to fall to shit, he might as well try to have something else lined up.

Bear took a sandwich in each hand and sat back down. He ate the first sandwich in three bites, then downed the second. He barely tasted it, but it felt good to have something solid in his stomach. Reaching for a third, he finally spoke. "All right, I'm listening."

"It's my understanding that you didn't have much of a choice in the matter when it came to your business arrangement with Malik."

Bear shrugged. "I guess."

"You protected George, who in turn suggested that his cousin take you under his wing. You're meant to protect George to pay off your debt. Is that correct?"

"More or less." Bear grabbed a few cubes of cheese. "What's your point?"

"My point is, you could do so much better than Malik." Kafka leaned forward. It was the first time Bear had seen fire in his eyes. He wanted this. Badly. "He might be a hot shot on Block 2, but when he ventures over here, he's at the bottom of the ladder."

"What are you suggesting?"

"Nothing yet. First, I need a show of good faith. I've got some plans in the works that will take Malik out of the picture and extend my reach into Block 2."

Bear sat up straight and made a show of looking around the room. "You got something to drink?"

Finally there was a flicker of annoyance that crossed Kafka's face, but it was gone as quickly as it had appeared. He stood up and walked to the back of the room, where he opened up a small pantry and took out a bottle of Coke. It was warm, but it was worth more than all the food put together.

Bear took a swig of the soda, but now he was paying attention. Kafka was pulling out all the stops for him. "Why work backwards? Block 2 is beneath you."

"Every general needs soldiers. Block 2 is ripe for the taking. They would kill, literally, to be employed by someone like me. I don't mind taking advantage of that."

"And where would I fit into this picture?"

"I'll need a bodyguard."

"You seem to have plenty already."

"You took out two of them," Kafka said. There was no anger in his voice. "So there's a couple openings."

"Let's say I'm interested," Bear said. "What's the show of good faith?"

Kafka leaned back in his chair and steepled his fingers. "I have a spy on the inside. He's been reliable so far, but I don't necessarily trust him. I want to make sure he's giving me good intel."

"So I spy on the spy?"

"It's as simple as that."

It was Bear's turn to laugh. He placed the half-empty Coke on the table and grabbed a couple more blocks of cheese. He popped one into his mouth. "Nothing is that simple. Malik employs me to watch out for his cousin. I failed at that today. He's also gonna know I met with you. Your spy will, too. Are you sure you thought this through?"

"Quite," Kafka replied. He picked up his tiny bell and rang it one more time. The same two men entered the room. Kafka stood up and Bear followed suit. The hairs on the back of his neck stood up. "I don't expect an answer right away, but regardless, I do have to ensure that both Malik and my spy don't suspect a thing. When you return to Block 2 with some decent bruises and tell him I offered to hire you and you refused, on account of your disinterest in prison politics, he'll be satisfied. Hell, he might even give you a raise."

Bear raised his fists. "Last time this didn't go too well for your men."

"I'm aware," Kafka said. He nodded toward the two figures in the doorway, who stepped aside to allow four more men inside the tiny room. Kafka backed up and out of the way. "Try not to break anything, boys. That goes for the table as well as his nose."

Chapter Ten

They didn't manage to avoid breaking the table, but Bear did walk out of there with his nose intact.

Then again, *walk* was a strong word. He was dragged out by two of Kafka's men and left limp and bleeding in the doorway between Blocks 2 and 3. Malik himself pulled Bear across the threshold and dumped him back in his bed. Bear could hear George moving on the bunk above him.

"What happened?" Malik demanded. Despite giving Bear the courtesy of being interrogated in his bed instead of the cold, hard ground, it sounded like Malik had no time for sympathy.

"Got jumped in the courtyard." Bear shifted and looked up at the bottom of the bed above him. "You doing okay, George?"

"Might've cracked a rib." His voice was weaker than usual. "But it would've been worse if you hadn't been there."

Bear closed his eyes and nodded to himself. The whole thing was a shitshow at this point, but at least George got out relatively unscathed. Despite the bloody mess he was in, he knew he'd heal up within a couple days.

Malik leaned closer and put a finger to Bear's chest. He didn't miss the way the other man chose to put pressure on one of the ripest bruises, but Bear didn't flinch. There was a wild rage behind Malik's eyes. He was afraid.

"Tell me everything."

Bear brushed aside Malik's hand and swiveled around to sit up on the edge of his bed. His head swam for a fraction of a second before righting itself. He vaguely wondered if he had a concussion but decided not to worry about it. Nothing he could do about it in here anyway. Block 2 didn't have an infirmary and he wasn't looking to go back to Block 3 any sooner than absolutely necessary.

"We were walking across the courtyard when we got jumped," Bear said. No use in telling Malik he hadn't been paying attention. Things were bad enough as it was. "George got thrown against the wall. Two guys came at me while a third did a number on George. Knocked one guy down, chased the third guy off, then took out the second guy."

"So why did George come back without you?" Malik asked. "Why wasn't his guard guarding him?"

Bear didn't have the energy to deal with cocky pieces of shit at any point in the day, but especially right now. Still, he bit his tongue. "Some asshole gave me a choice. I could either follow him and let his men return George to you, or I could try taking on the entire courtyard. The decision was pretty easy, actually."

Malik ground his teeth together before he spoke again. "Who was it?"

"Some guy named Kafka."

Malik stood up so suddenly, Bear's body tensed, ready for another fight. But Malik wasn't looking at him. Instead, he marched out of the cell and returned a few minutes later with Hassan.

"Tell us everything that happened with Kafka," Malik demanded.

Hassan looked between Bear and Malik with wide eyes. "Kafka? He saw Kafka?"

Malik nodded but didn't say anything. He gestured for Bear to continue.

Bear returned Hassan's gaze. The other man's body was taut, like he was ready to sprint away. There was an uneasy energy there, but he was working to keep his face as devoid of emotion as possible. Was Hassan terrified of Kafka? The guy exuded a certain amount of power in just how he dressed, with his button-down shirt and his slacks, but in a fight he wouldn't be much trouble.

Unless the reason for Hassan's fear wasn't what scared him so much. Maybe it was what Kafka could reveal about Hassan.

"He invited me to lunch," Bear said casually. He looked at Malik when he spoke, but he was keeping an eye on Hassan's reactions.

Malik growled. "Don't play with me, man. What did he offer you?"

Bear shifted on the bed and winced. Maybe he had a cracked rib, too. "Said he had a business proposition." Bear paused. How much did he want to reveal in front of Hassan, just in case he was Kafka's man on the inside? "He told me he could get me into Block 3 to be his personal guard."

Malik was as high strung as Bear had ever seen him. "In return for what?"

"Information on you."

Malik froze. "What's Kafka want with me? We don't butt heads. I'm not interested in him."

"He's interested in you, though. He knows George is your cousin. He said the only reason why we got those jobs in the kitchen was because he allowed it. Sounds like your men might not be your men after all."

Malik's eyes narrowed. It was a jab to his pride to be sure, but it was also reality. Alliances changed on a dime within prison walls. "What did you tell him?"

"Same thing I told you," Bear said. "No interest in prison politics."

"And he just let you go?"

Bear gestured to his bruised and bloody body. "Obviously not."

"He could've had you killed. He didn't. Why?"

"Hell if I know." Bear shifted and groaned again. "Maybe to give me a chance to reconsider. He clearly doesn't know me very well."

Malik was silent for several beats. He made his way toward the cell door, Hassan close on his heels, but paused and looked back at Bear. "I won't forget your loyalty."

Then he left, with Hassan throwing one last look over his shoulder before they disappeared out of view.

Bear barely slept that night. The bed was uncomfortable enough on its own, but his bruised ribs weren't making it any easier. He was fairly certain they weren't broken, but they were sore at any rate.

Still, he was expected to go back to work the next day, and he did. Even George crawled out of bed, moaning softly. But it was the only sound he made. They both knew they had been lucky enough to walk away with their lives, so it seemed pointless to complain.

Despite the fogginess swirling around inside Bear's head, he kept a sharp eye out as soon as he stepped through to Block 3. The courtyard was back to its normal bustle of activity, and nothing in particular seemed out of place.

Still, Bear spotted the boxer from the day before looking over at him from a group of three men. Their postures were relaxed, but it still made Bear tighten his hands into fists. There was no sign of the bald man, but he caught sight of the thin one who had jumped George, slipping through a doorway into one of the wings.

Kafka was absent, though Bear wasn't surprised. He didn't mingle with the common folk out in the courtyard unless he was putting on a show like he did yesterday. He was probably tucked away in his little apartment, sipping Coke and reading a good book. Or else planning how he was going to take over Block 2 without causing suspicion with his own block leader.

Hassan had to be Kafka's spy. Malik didn't keep anyone else close, and the only reason why he felt comfortable enough trusting the other man in the first place was because they both had nukes aimed at each other. If Hassan decided to fire his weapons, Malik would return the volley and they'd both be taken out.

But if Hassan could get Kafka on his side, that would tip the balance in his favor. Together, they could take Malik out of the equation and Hassan would be the new Block 2 leader. Meanwhile, Kafka would have someone indebted to him sitting on the throne in Block 2. When he wanted to make his move to take over Block 3, he'd have an army to back him up.

It was a dangerous game. Kafka would have to convince his own block leader that this move would actually work out in both of their favors. Maybe the real plan was taking over Block 4. Bear hadn't heard much about it since not many people could afford to pay the toll to cross over into the last section of the prison, but from what he knew, they all lived like kings over there.

Bear was occupied by the chess board currently laid out in his mind. He never meant to get wrapped up in other people's vendettas, but that had been the case since Sophia and Derek were killed. The universe clearly thought his vacation should be over. But why did the realities of life have to set in so hard?

Not for the first time, Bear thought of Jack. He hoped everything was okay with his friend. He couldn't blame him for not picking up the phone, but the fact that there hadn't even been a voicemail wasn't sitting right with him. Maybe Jack was in trouble. Or maybe he just didn't want to be found, even by Bear. Either way, the only way Bear was getting out of the St. Lucian Rehabilitation Center was if the universe decided to cut him a break.

Sometimes it's funny how Fate decides to play its hand.

One minute Bear was sitting across from George, eating his usual slop, and the next he was being hauled to his feet by a pair of inmates even bigger than him. They had pulled his arms behind his back so suddenly and with such force, that he couldn't get out of their grip. His bruised ribs and sore shoulders didn't exactly work in his favor.

George hopped up like he was gonna make a run for it back to Block 2 to get his cousin, but Bear shook his head. If someone wanted to speak to him so badly, he'd listen to what they had to say and hoped it ended in fewer bruises than yesterday. He didn't like the idea of being used for someone else's gain, but it was becoming increasingly obvious that keeping his head down and going with the flow was going to allow him to live the longest.

Still, he wasn't looking forward to whatever came next. He didn't recognize the men, and he doubted they were Kafka's. The man he'd met yesterday appeared to be a little more subtle than this. He was a businessman. Forcibly summoning someone you saw as a potential avenue for gaining more power wasn't a smart business move.

Bear also doubted this was Malik's way of making a move. Showing his hand like this in someone else's territory was bound to get him in trouble one way or another. No, it was much more likely he was about to come face to face with Kafka's block leader.

Great, Bear thought. *One more person putting me in a spotlight I've actively been trying to avoid.*

When the two men spun him around, Bear came face to face with a third. Before Bear could even tighten his stomach muscles and prepare for the blow, the third man struck him in the solar plexus and knocked the wind out of him. Bear's knees gave out, but the two men holding him didn't let him drop to the ground.

The third man, who seemed to be the leader of the trio, bent down to look Bear in the eyes. "You're one lucky bastard, you know that, right?" he whispered. Bear doubted anyone could hear him, not even his two lackeys. "But I'm not gonna let any of these guys know that. I'd apologize, but I'm gonna enjoy this too much to mean it."

This time Bear saw the wind-up coming, but he was still trying to suck in air. One blow landed to the side of his face, while the other hit him square on the jaw. Blood started to trickle down from the corner of his right brow, and just when he started to gain some of his breath back, the man struck him in the stomach one more time.

The courtyard had gathered to watch, and when there was a sufficient amount of witnesses and blood, Bear was dragged forward. But he wasn't led through one of the Block 3 wings. Instead, he was forced through the door back into Block 2.

Malik emerged from his cell where he had been lying comfortably. Despite one swollen eye, Bear still saw that there was a girl in there with him. It was another luxury you could get within the prison walls if you had enough money.

"What's going on?" Malik asked. "Where are you taking my guy?"

"Not your guy anymore," the leader said. "Say your goodbyes."

Bear tried to struggle, but the two lackeys just pinched his arms back another couple inches and he went limp again. He could feel his muscles stretching to capacity, and the last thing he needed was to tear something and really not be able to defend himself.

It didn't become clear where they were taking him until they passed back through Block 1. All the inmates left out here watched as he was dragged from one end to the other with no regards for their makeshift shelters. Bear heard some grumblings here and there, but no one dared to move against the small group tearing through the courtyard.

Once they left the prison walls, the two men holding Bear walked him a few feet forward and unceremoniously dumped him on the ground. There were a few chuckles behind him, presumably from the officers, but otherwise no one said anything. The three inmates turned on their heels and left Bear kneeling in the dirt.

It wasn't until he heard the gate close behind that reality set in.

He was free.

Chapter Eleven

"And here I thought you couldn't get uglier, Bear."

The voice was familiar, but he couldn't decide if it was just his mind playing tricks on him. He turned toward the sound, which originated about a dozen feet off to his left. A silver truck sat in the grass, the engine running. The bright, mid-day sun reflected off the side door, blinding Bear until he put a hand up to shield his eyes.

It took a moment, but finally the figure came into focus. As soon as he did, Bear was on his feet and reaching for a weapon that wasn't there. He froze, but stood his ground, trying to decide if it was suicide to attack with nothing more than his fists and a couple bruised ribs.

"I don't think you'd win," the other man said.

"What the Sam hell are you doing here Thorne?"

Thorne chuckled and pushed off the side of the truck. He had the balls to walk right up to Bear and hold out his hand like they were old friends. "I come in peace."

Bear refused to shake. "You'll forgive me if I don't quite believe that."

Thorne put his hand back in his pocket, a movement that Bear didn't miss. Thorne shook his head. "I know you don't believe this, but I really am here under a white flag."

"And why is that?" Bear asked. "The last time I saw you, there were snipers looking to blow a hole in my chest."

"Fair enough," Thorne said. "But I need your help."

Bear was silent for a beat. Then he threw his head back and laughed long and loud. Much longer and louder than necessary. But it felt good to expel that energy. It felt good to shove his disbelief in Thorne's face. "You've got to be kidding."

"I'm not," Thorne said. "But I'd rather discuss it away from here."

"You're an idiot if you think I'm going anywhere with you."

Thorne looked like he wanted to take a step closer, to really get in Bear's face, but thought better of it. He was already in striking range. There was no need to make himself an even easier target. "You'd be an idiot if you didn't listen to what I have to say."

Bear held out his hands. "I am listening."

Thorne sighed, his gaze flickering over Bear's shoulder to look at the guards. He lowered his voice. "I'm the one who got you out of here, you know. You should be thanking me."

"How'd you even know where I was?"

Thorne straightened up. He just couldn't help looking like a cocky bastard. It was his default setting. "I tracked your phone call to Jack."

Bear grabbed the front of Thorne's shirt, happy to get a little sweat and blood on it. "Where is he? What'd you do to him?"

Thorne removed Bear's hand from his collar and smoothed out his shirt, looking down at the blood with disdain. "Jack's fine. Or, at least, I assume he's fine. It appears he's a little better at flying under the radar than you are."

"So you have no idea where he is?"

"Not a clue."

"That's one point in your favor." Bear squinted his eyes against the sun. "Still doesn't explain how you found me."

"Like I said, I tracked your phone call to Jack. He never got it, by the way. I figure he knew I had tapped the line and killed the number. Realized you were calling from a jail on St. Lucia and figured you got yourself in a tight spot. I dropped some money in the judge's lap and got them to set you free."

"And I'm supposed to trust that you're not gonna kill me as soon as I get in that truck with you?" Bear asked.

Thorne rolled his eyes. "If I wanted to have you killed, I would've just paid one of the prisoners to do it. Would've been a hell of a lot cheaper."

"Some guys like to pull the trigger themselves," Bear said. "You strike me as one of those guys."

"You're not wrong." Thorne sighed heavily. "Look, I know you think I'm a bastard, Bear, but I'm not as terrible as you've been led to believe."

"So, what? I'm supposed to think you did this out of the kindness of your heart?"

"Like I said, I need your help." Thorne crossed his arms over his chest. "But I'm not going to discuss details out here. You can either get in the truck or go back to your cell."

Bear didn't like either option, but now that he was outside the prison walls, he didn't want to go back in. Thorne appeared to be by himself, and despite their history, this wouldn't be the first time he let Bear walk away from an encounter with him. If Thorne wanted him dead, he had no doubt in his mind that he would've already made it happen.

"Fine," Bear said. "But I need to do one last thing."

Bear didn't bother explaining. He just spun on his heel and

walked back to the prison entrance. The guards both put their hands on their guns but didn't draw them. One stepped forward.

"Don't do anything you're gonna regret."

Bear held up his hands. "That's the plan. Are you Davis?"

The man nodded.

"Can you get a message to Malik for me?"

Davis smiled. "What's in it for me?"

Bear looked over his shoulder at Thorne, who rolled his eyes and stepped forward. He reached into his pocket but stopped short of pulling anything out. "If I do this, you'll help me?"

"I'll listen to what you have to say," Bear corrected. "That's about as good as it's gonna get for now."

Either Thorne was unconcerned or desperate, but either way he pulled a wad of bills out of his pocket and stuffed them into the guard's hand.

Davis tipped his head and put the money in his pocket, then turned toward Bear and waited.

"Tell Malik Bear says not to trust Hassan."

Davis blinked. "That's it? That's all you want to say?"

"It'll get the job done," Bear said.

"Works for me." Davis turned back to the gate and called one of the inmates forward.

Bear started walking toward Thorne's truck. Either Malik would get the message or he wouldn't. Bear wasn't going to waste time standing around wondering.

When he reached the passenger side door, he stopped. Thorne got in and looked at him expectantly.

Bear stared him down. "You know I still don't trust you."

"I don't exactly trust you either," Thorne said. "But I don't have a choice in the matter."

Bear sighed. He didn't like the idea of climbing into a car with Thorne without at least having an idea of what's going on.

Thorne must've seen the hesitation on his face. "I'll explain everything shortly. But I want to get out of here before someone starts asking questions."

Bear looked back at the prison one last time, then got in the truck and slammed the door shut after him. "Fine. But I never did get to have my lunch." He looked at Thorne with a shit-eating grin on his face. "You're buying."

Chapter Twelve

Thorne drove about a mile before he pulled off the side of the road and told Bear they were ditching the truck. By this time Bear had grown too curious to complain. He wanted to know what Thorne was up to and he currently didn't have any other option than to go with the flow.

They walked another quarter mile before a navy blue Volkswagen Golf from the '80s appeared around the bend. As they approached, Bear noticed a small bald-headed man sitting in the front seat. Bear looked at Thorne out of the corner of his eye, but the other man didn't look concerned. Instead, Thorne opened the rear driver's side door and gestured for Bear to get in, forcing him to slide over when he joined him in the back seat.

Without prompting, the driver turned the key in the ignition and slowly pulled out onto the road, making his way back into town. His head was covered in a sheen of sweat, but otherwise he looked completely unbothered. Bear turned to Thorne expectantly.

"His name's Giovanni," Thorne said. "Good driver. Quiet guy."

"Fascinating," Bear said. "And not the kind of information I was looking for."

"Lunch first," Thorne replied, turning toward his window and watching the trees speed by. "Then we'll talk."

Bear forced himself to relax. He could do some serious damage from his position beside Thorne, but the other man seemed unconcerned. Bear didn't go as far as closing his eyes, but he let them glaze over as they took the twists and turns in the road at a moderate speed.

They were at the edge of a small town when Giovanni pulled over near a food stand. The smell of cooking meat made Bear's mouth water and his stomach grumble. This was a whole other playing field even compared to the feast he had with Kafka just yesterday. He hoped his stomach could handle the decadence.

Thorne didn't have to be prompted this time. He paid for all three meals and the man inside the small hut handed them their food before Bear's stomach could rumble a second time. Bear had decided on Lambi—conch made into fritters—and fried plantains. It was salty, fresh, filling, and just what he needed after two weeks surviving on prison food.

Bear and Thorne returned to the car and leaned up against the hood. It was warm after their drive, but Bear didn't care. Everything felt new and bright out here. He forced himself to eat slowly, despite his growling stomach. He wanted to remember every bite, every burst of flavor. Sophia would've loved how rich his Lambi tasted, but he tried not to dwell on that either.

Giovanni walked off down the road, enjoying his sandwich and looking completely at ease. Bear turned toward Thorne expectantly. He didn't want to wait any longer for some answers.

"What?" Thorne asked.

Bear sighed. He also didn't want to play games. "Just tell me what's going on, Thorne. What am I getting myself into?"

Thorne took a big bite of his sandwich and chewed thoughtfully. The only thing keeping Bear from launching himself at the other man was the fact that he still had half his Lambi left. No way was he going to waste food just to get into a fist fight with some asshole.

Finally, Thorne swallowed and wiped his mouth with a napkin. Then he turned to Bear and cleared his throat. "Costa Rica set off a shitstorm that even I'm having trouble cleaning up."

"Not my problem."

"You were involved in that mess as much as I was. You have a responsibility here."

Bear threw his head back and laughed. A few people turned in their direction. He didn't care. "You have some balls talking to me about responsibility, Thorne. I don't owe you shit."

Thorne tossed the remainder of his sandwich on the ground where a stray dog immediately snatched it up. "You want to go back to prison, Bear? You'll rot in there."

"I'll find a way out." Bear finished the rest of his meal. The stray dog looked at him mournfully and then padded off. "I've been in worse scrapes before. Besides, I'd rather not owe you one. Might get me stabbed in the back."

Thorne sighed, and then rubbed a hand down his face. He looked tired—no, *exhausted*. How much did Costa Rica take out of him? How bad was it, really? Bear was curious, but he wasn't about to open those flood gates.

"I'm sorry about your friends," Thorne said.

Bear didn't think. He just reacted. One minute he was standing there with an empty plate in his hand, and the next he had Thorne by the collar. "Don't you disrespect them."

Thorne put his hands up in surrender. Bear knew well and good Thorne could've taken him down in a dozen different ways, but he didn't. Bear remembered the snipers that had set their sights on him the last time he saw Thorne and let go of the other man. He took a couple steps back and scanned the treeline.

"There's no one out there other than Giovanni." Thorne smoothed out his shirt. "Look, I know something about the shooting and I'd rather not get punched in the face for it."

Bear studied Thorne for a moment. There was nothing more he'd like to do than put a bullet in this man's head, but he wasn't sure it would be worth it. Thorne was a smart guy. He'd have backup, regardless. For all Bear knew, Giovanni was a deadly assassin just waiting for Bear to try to take his boss out. The most dangerous of enemies came in the most deceptive packages.

"No guarantee," Bear said. "But I'll attempt to restrain myself."

"Fair enough." Thorne paused again, as if weighing his chances one last time. "The hit on the bar? It wasn't meant for them."

"I figured that out already, genius. There was no one on that island that didn't love or respect them."

"It was meant for you."

Bear froze. It's not that the idea was out of the realm of possibility. He had pissed off a lot of people in the past, so it was only a matter of time before that caught up to him. What was surprising was that Bear had never considered it. And why would he? No one on the island knew who he really was, and those who did know his identity couldn't have known his location.

Thorne had only been able to find him after Bear had made a call to Jack, and he practically had unlimited resources at his fingertips.

Bear looked up at Thorne. "Who?"

"I don't know yet. I'm still working on that. But these guys are serious, Bear. How long have you been off the grid and I couldn't find you? Good job on that, by the way."

"I don't need your approval, Thorne."

"I'm well aware of that. It was just a compliment." Thorne pushed off the car and turned in a circle, checking his surroundings. "Look, I know you don't like me, but whether you want to believe it or not, you're as mixed up in all of this as I am. They're gonna keep coming after you until you're dead. Or until you wished you were."

"Thanks for the advice. I guess I'll be heading out then." Bear turned around and starting walking off in the other direction. He half expected an assault team to burst out of the trees and try to stop him, but he didn't care. He was done with the games. "No point in sticking around if they know where I am. Always wanted to go on a world tour."

"So, what? You're just gonna keep running?" Thorne called out after him. "Moving from place to place every couple weeks? What kind of life is that?"

"One that I'm used to," Bear said. "Have a good life, Thorne. Hope you get shot in the back real soon."

"Bear." Thorne's voice was distant but still discernible. If Bear didn't know any better, he'd say the man almost sounded desperate. "Bear, they've got Sadie."

Chapter Thirteen

Bear was in one of his least favorite places in the entire world: a plane. It was a private jet with all the amenities and plenty of room for his large frame, but it didn't matter how many bells and whistles the thing had, it was still a plane. And Bear still felt like he was going to see his Lambi again. So he closed his eyes, controlled his breathing, and focused on what was going to happen once his feet hit solid ground again.

As soon as Bear had heard Sadie's name, his brain short-circuited. One minute he was a couple dozen yards away from Thorne, ready to track down Jack no matter how much time it took, and the next minute he was on top of the source of all his problems, pummeling the man's face in.

On the bright side, Thorne really was telling the truth about there not being snipers hiding out in the trees around him. Giovanni didn't appear to be a secret assassin either, but he did attempt to pull Bear off his boss to no effect.

It took three locals to pull Bear away from Thorne, and that was enough to calm him down. As much as he talked about not caring, he really didn't want to go back to jail. He had no doubt he'd be able to get out again, but that sort of time behind bars changes a person. And it's not like Bear had many friends on the inside, especially after what just went down with Kafka and Malik.

Thorne had shielded his face and avoided the blows the best he could without striking back, but he still had a busted lip and blood was trickling from the corner of his right eyebrow. He had gotten to his feet and waved off the locals. "He just got some bad news."

The guys just shrugged and let the two walk back toward their car. Bear was still fuming, but he was satisfied with the couple of licks he had gotten on Thorne. It would have to satiate him for now.

The plane jostled a little up and down, and Bear gripped the armrests until his fingers hurt. He didn't bother opening his eyes. It would just make matters worse. He pressed his feet down to remind himself there was something under him, but it didn't help. He felt every inch of the open air between him and the earth. Gravity was stronger up here.

Bear took a deep breath and went over the information Thorne had provided him. It wasn't much. He refused to say who had Sadie, even when Bear had threatened more fists to the face. But Thorne had held fast, saying he wasn't sure and he didn't want to send Bear out on a wild goose chase. More people would get hurt that way.

Bear didn't believe a word Thorne said. He was conniving and manipulative and didn't give a rat's ass who got hurt in the process. There was a reason why Thorne was refusing to tell him the truth, but Bear wasn't going to get it out of him. The only solution was to play the game until Thorne made a wrong move or Bear found Sadie on his own.

The only piece of information Thorne gave Bear was that he needed to go to Hong Kong to meet a contact. He refused to say why and eventually Bear just stopped asking. He had started getting antsy thinking of where Sadie could possibly be and what they could possibly be doing to her. She could hold her own—she had proven that in Costa Rica—but humans were fragile creatures. Depending on what she was going through, either her body or her mind would give out. It was only a matter of time.

Bear took another deep breath, but this one wasn't because of the plane. He thought he'd processed everything that had happened to him up until this point. He'd had plenty of downtime behind bars, after all. But the sting of Derek and Sophia's death was still sharp. And now Sadie had been taken. Because of him.

Not for the first time, Bear wondered who could have taken her. Thorne had said this was a result of what went down in Costa Rica. Then again, the last time Bear had seen him, Thorne had made a not-so-veiled threat about Sadie's whereabouts. Instinct told him Thorne was hiding something, but logic told him it wouldn't make sense to kidnap Sadie just to send Bear out to find her again.

There must be something Bear was missing, but he wouldn't be able to put the puzzle together without more data.

Bear had last seen Sadie in the airport as all three of them flew out of Costa Rica. She had told Jack that she wasn't going to do any more undercover missions any time soon. That didn't mean she wouldn't still be throwing herself into a lion's den once or twice, but her ops would be a lot more short-lived.

So where had Sadie been when she was taken? At home? At work? Out on a mission? Thorne hadn't provided any of those details, but hopefully his contact in Hong Kong would be able to. Bear didn't give a shit about the problems Thorne was facing right now, but he did give a shit about Sadie. For now, those two issues were one in the same, but as soon as Bear figured out where Sadie was, he'd get her out of there and they'd both track down Jack together. Maybe they could even pretend they were all just old friends for a couple of days.

The fantasy was nice, but Bear wouldn't let himself have too much hope. First things first. One foot in front of the other.

Bear rifled through the list of people they had dealt with in Costa Rica. Vasquez had a grudge against Jack since Jack had broken his nose the last time they saw each other. Bear didn't think Vasquez had the power to pull off something quite like this, but it was always dangerous to underestimate your opponents.

As for anyone else wanting a piece of Bear? Who knows. He'd made plenty of enemies over the years. As had Jack. This might not even be about Bear at all. Maybe it was about Noble and his practically non-existent relationship with Sadie.

Bear kept mulling over the names of anyone he might have gotten into it with in the past. Frank Skinner's name popped up more than once. He trusted the guy even less than Jack did, but this didn't quite have his signature on it. The last they saw of Frank, he was working on a way to track down Thorne. He'd been double-crossed and a man like Skinner didn't forget about that easily. Chances were he was still looking under every rock for Thorne. Too bad Bear had no way of calling him in at the moment. The look on Thorne's face would be priceless.

But it wouldn't be worth it if he lost track of Sadie in the process. It was better to just keep his head down, and that's what Bear did until the plane hit the tarmac in Hong Kong. The final descent was always the worst, even in a private jet. That moment when the wheels finally touched the ground felt like death every single time, but a sense of relief always followed it, and there was no greater feeling than that.

Chapter Fourteen

The flight from St. Lucia to Hong Kong was twenty-four hours long, with one stop in Atlanta and another in Seattle. Bear would've preferred the straight-shot right to Hong Kong, since it would mean fewer takeoffs and landings, but the universe just wasn't looking out for him these days.

When he finally did make it to Hong Kong, his legs were tight, his back was sore, and his hands felt like they were full of arthritis. He did his best to stretch everything out on his way through the airport, but he had a feeling the only thing that would help was a hot shower and a good bed.

Thorne had set him up with a fake name and passport. Something generic. He told the customs officers he was there on business, and it was a good thing Thorne had gotten him a suit, too. The man looked him up and down with a raised eyebrow but didn't bother asking too many questions. He stamped the book and motioned him on.

Bear wasn't due to meet Thorne's contact until later that afternoon, so he checked into a hotel in the downtown area. It felt strange to be around so many people after having been stationed on an island for a couple months, but the change in pace felt good. The energy of the city recharged him.

Bear still stood out wherever he went, but with businessmen and women rushing from one place to the next, no one paid him any mind. Sometimes the best place to hide was right in the middle of the crowd.

Bear allowed himself the luxury of a suite. He had the money and he wasn't looking forward to spending any amount of time in a hotel room the size of his old jail cell. Besides, he didn't know what he was getting himself into. In a few days' time, he could be camping out in the middle of the woods with mud smeared across his face. Might as well indulge while he could.

Bear took the stairs instead of the elevator. It got his blood pumping. It felt good to get some cardio in after all that time sitting on a plane, and he felt his muscles start to loosen. The hot shower that followed did the rest of the work. By the time he was dry and dressed in something a bit more casual, he was ready to jump into whatever mess Thorne had created for him.

Bear sat on a bench in a park in downtown Hong Kong. The sky was clear with a few clouds whipping past on the outer fringes. The sun smacked his forehead. The warmth spread down his face, around his neck, down his torso. The slight breeze kept him from getting too hot. Children played a couple dozen yards from him, and every once in a while a businessman or woman would walk by, their phone held to their head, speaking quickly and quietly.

Thorne had told Bear his contact would approach him, but that didn't stop Bear from trying to peg the person the moment they came into view. Not that he had any information to go on. Thorne had only told him it was someone they could get information from. He hadn't said who they were or what their background was. Come to think of it, he hadn't even said it was someone they could trust.

Bear shifted on the hard, wooden bench and caught sight of a fairly average looking Asian man. He was on the phone, but his mouth never moved. His gaze was constantly roaming, however, and as soon as it landed on Bear, he looked away. Most of the people around here couldn't help but stare at the large, obviously American man enjoying the day in the park. This had to be the guy.

A minute later the man sat down on the other side of the bench. He looked around for a moment before speaking to Bear without removing his phone from the side of his head. He was pale with dark eyebrows and shaggy hair. There was something unsettling about his face that Bear couldn't quite put his finger on. He looked like he'd sooner set you on fire than actually throw a punch. Bear didn't trust people who weren't up for a fair fight.

"Are you Mr. Logan?"

Bear stared straight ahead. He'd played this game before. "I am."

"My name is Cheung." He paused to force a cough. "Thorne tells me I can trust you."

"Funny," Bear said. "He didn't say the same about you."

The other man laughed, but it sounded more like a hiss. "Thorne and I aren't friends. We have a business arrangement."

"You're here to provide me with information."

Cheung looked away again before answering. "Yes."

Bear kept his gaze level and straight ahead watching the reflection of a jet in the mirrored glass of a high-rise. "And what is Thorne providing you?"

"That is between Thorne and myself." Cheung stood up and smoothed his blazer. "Follow me at a distance. We don't want to look suspicious."

"I've done this once or twice, Cheung. No need to hold my hand."

Cheung didn't answer. Instead, he set off back from where he came. Bear scanned the park but didn't see anyone paying attention to him, so he stood and followed Cheung at a slightly slower pace. They followed the winding pathways for ten minutes. Every time Bear lost sight of the other man, he'd find him at the next bend, looking at a tree or a flower with feigned interest until Bear was close enough again.

Eventually they came to a gated tunnel underneath a bridge. Cheung placed his phone into his pocket and pulled out a small silver key. He unlocked the gate and slipped inside without looking back. Bear hesitated before following. If Cheung wanted a secluded area to take Bear out, this would do perfectly.

Bear zeroed in on the feeling of a 9mm pistol tucked inside the waist of his pants. He had to go through customs when he landed, but Thorne had paid off a few people to guarantee his bags got waved through. Inside were a few weapons with a bit more firepower, but Bear figured he'd look a little suspicious carrying an assault rifle through the park, so he'd settled on the handgun.

Despite his reservations, Bear opened the gate wide enough to enter and walked down the dark tunnel until he found another door. This one was slightly ajar, and when he pushed it open, it squeaked on its rusted hinges. The smell of mold filled the air. He paused here for a moment, listening for any sounds on the other side. There was the *drip, drip, drip* of water and a *click clack* of what sounded like keys. As far as he could tell, Cheung was the only person in the room.

So, without drawing his weapon, Bear pushed the door open the rest of the way and entered the room. It was cold, damp, and dark. On top of a small metal desk with rusted feet sat a dim desk lamp and a boxy laptop. A thin layer of dust covered the surface. Cheung stood in front of it, with his back to the door.

He was either incredibly confident or incredibly stupid. Maybe both.

Cheung continued tapping on the keyboard long enough for Bear to get annoyed enough to clear his throat. The other man paused for a few seconds, like his train of thought had been interrupted, and then continued typing away.

"Look, man, I'm in a bit of a hurry," Bear said. "Let's get this over with."

Tap, tap, tap.

After another excruciating minute, Cheung turned around with a smile on his face. It did him no favors, and Bear realized he couldn't peg which side of the law this man was on. He was twitchy like a criminal, but cocky like an agent. Maybe he was a little bit of both. Corruption ran deep all over the world.

"You're to retrieve a package from what will likely be a heavily fortified house—"

"Wait a second." Bear stepped forward. Cheung didn't flinch, but the smile did drop off his face. "I'm here to receive information from you, not do your dirty work."

"This is not my dirty work," Cheung said, spreading his arms wide. "This is the information you need. If you don't want it, you can tell Thorne I'm still charging him."

Bear pinched the bridge of his nose. He didn't have time for this but wringing this guy's neck would just waste even more of it. "What's in the package?"

"The information you need."

Bear growled. "If you say that one more time—"

Cheung held up his hands in surrender, but there was a smile twitching around the corners of his mouth. "I only know what I'm told."

"Then you better talk fast," Bear said. He had an urge to wipe the smile off Cheung's face with the butt of his pistol. "Start from the beginning."

Cheung stepped to the side of the boxy laptop, revealing a simple map of a suburb outside Hong Kong. The houses were clustered together, which would make approaching one without being seen extremely difficult—especially for Bear.

"This is the house you'll need." Cheung hit a key and the map was replaced with a satellite shot of a plain two-story home. He hit another key and a blueprint of the house popped up. "The package will be in the northeast bedroom on the second floor. The mission is fairly straightforward: enter the house, dispatch anyone who stands in your way, retrieve the package, and return here."

Bear studied the blueprint. "Why does this feel like it won't be as easy as it sounds?"

"Because it won't." Cheung wore that smile again, the one that twisted his face into something you just wanted to hit. "This is one of the safe houses for a criminal syndicate who has more power in Hong Kong than the government. They have enough money to do whatever they want and enough guns to make sure that if you can't be bought, you can be killed."

"Great." Bear took a step back and scratched his chin. "You got anything that can help with that? I came unarmed."

Cheung laughed. "I wouldn't recommend lying to me, Mr. Logan. I'm smarter than you look."

"Thank Christ for that."

"My job is to provide information, not firepower. You'll need to get that on your own."

"Your job isn't to provide information. It's to provide an opportunity for information."

Cheung's shrug was slow and unconcerned. "That's how it works here."

Bear leaned back against the wall, finding a wisp of cool air blowing down from a vent. "Seems like you got the easy part of the job."

"How do you think I've stayed alive for so long?"

"Honestly, I'm surprised you've made it this far without that shit-eating grin of yours getting you into trouble."

"I've been in plenty of trouble, Mr. Logan. It's why I'm so adept at getting out of it."

Bear laughed. "On that, Mr. Cheung, at least we can relate."

Chapter Fifteen

Bear sat in the brand-new Nissan Altima he had rented before leaving the city. It had tinted windows dark enough to hide his figure and the rucksack on the seat next to him filled with enough firepower to take on a small gang. He had to wait until nightfall to hit the house, but the itch to do something nagged at him. Every minute Sadie was left on her own was another chance that she could be dead.

Or worse.

And he didn't want to consider worse.

It was easy to forget he wasn't in the suburbs in some affluent town in America instead of right outside Hong Kong. All the houses were the same cookie-cutter bullshit until you looked closer and saw the little details that reminded him he was a long way from home. Everything pristine and orderly. Good luck charms hanging from the front doors. The intense realization it would not be hard to track him down based on word-of-mouth descriptions alone smacked him in the gut.

The rental turned out to be the right choice. He saw at least six others on this street alone, never mind the countless ones he had passed on his way here. If anyone looked in his direction, all they would see was one of their neighbors' cars parked on the street. It was the only kind of camouflage Bear had right now. He'd have to wait until night fell before he could do anything on foot.

The street was quiet. Almost pleasant. The weather a perfect mix of warm and breezy. Bear had cracked the window and felt himself being lulled into a state of complacent relaxation. The sweet smell of a flower bed drifted into the cabin.

The moment his thoughts drifted, he rolled up the window and blasted the air. He couldn't afford to let this opportunity slip through his fingers.

Worse yet, Sadie couldn't afford it.

He had parked down the road from his target, between two houses with no cars in their driveways. He figured whoever lived there would be gone for the day and wouldn't report a strange car sitting outside their home. It provided him enough distance to be safe, but he was close enough to see all the comings and goings of the people who were somehow inexplicably tied to Sadie's kidnapping. And there was plenty of data to sift through. It seemed like every half hour, at least, someone was either arriving or departing from the house. They were mostly men, but some women as well. Most of the men were dressed in suits, dark gray, black, or blue. A few here and there stood out—burgundy, green, even one that was dark orange. These were the important guys. The ones who didn't mind being a little flashy. The ones that could afford to stand out.

Then again, maybe they were idiots who didn't realize any attention is negative.

The women were a different story. Most of them were in short skirts or dresses, with boots and shiny jackets and jewelry visible even from his distant vantage point. He wasn't sure if they were prostitutes or the girlfriends of the men who were coming and going. Some of them walked in with their heads held high, but more than one stumbled their way up the steps and through the front door.

Cheung hadn't told him what was going on in the house, other than it was a safe space for members of the criminal syndicate using it.

Bear chuckled, thinking of the rude awakening they were going to get when he kicked down their door.

But the women were a wild card he hadn't counted on. It was one thing to take down someone who had made the mistake of aiming a firearm in his direction. And even though Cheung told him to dispatch anyone in his way, Bear couldn't pull the trigger on somebody who was just trying to survive this mess of a world.

When the first neighbor pulled into their driveway Bear waited ten minutes and then eased away from the curb. He took a short drive around the neighborhood, careful not to cross in front of the safehouse and draw any attention to himself. Cheung hadn't indicated that anyone in the neighborhood was on the payroll, but Bear wasn't going to take chances.

By the time the sun set, Bear was on the opposite end of the street, parked at the corner and as far out of the way as he could be while still keeping an eye on the house. He couldn't stop himself from looking at the clock every two or three minutes thinking at least ten had passed. Sadie's face kept pushing its way to the forefront of his mind, pleading with him to hurry up. That she didn't have much time. Bear knew it was guilt playing with his head, but it didn't make him any less antsy.

The constant reminder caused something inside to snap. He had one foot on the pavement and was halfway out of the car when an SUV with windows as dark as his pulled up in front of the house. Four doors whipped open. Six men exited the vehicle.

Bear saw the man in the burgundy suit again. From this angle he looked even more impressive. He wore gold chains around his neck and a gold watch on his wrist. If Bear had to put money down, he'd bet this was one of the heads of the organization.

Bear slowly shifted his body weight and folded himself back into the Nissan not quite closing the door behind him. It was dark but there were plenty of street lights. The men escorting the burgundy suit into the house kept their heads on a swivel, taking in the street—including Bear's Altima.

One of the men broke free from the group, calling over his shoulder. Bear imagined he was telling the others that he was going to check out the car parked in the darkest corner of the road just to make sure it was empty. The five other men kept on a line walking their boss into the house, where they were greeted with cheers that even Bear could hear.

Bear tugged his door shut until it clicked and leaned his seat down, tossing the duffel bag full of weapons into the back. He closed his eyes and folded his hands over his chest and pretended to be asleep. It was a risk. Hell, remaining there was a risk. But he was hoping everyone in that house was more interested in keeping a low profile than making an example out of him.

A minute passed. And then another. Bear breathed deep and rhythmic despite his pounding heart. He didn't like being exposed like this—belly up and waiting for someone else to make the first move. He was just about to open his eyes a crack when there was a solid knock on his window.

Bear started awake, looking around and pretending to wipe the sleep from his eyes. He looked up at the man outside his door and raised his hand to give him a moment while he readjusted his seat. Then he cracked the window and gave the man a sheepish smile.

"What seems to be the problem?" Bear asked.

The man looked down at him with dark eyes. He was tall and lean with his long hair pulled back into a bun. An earpiece protruded from the side of his head. "What are you doing here?"

"I'm sorry?" Bear asked, furrowing his brow and pretending he couldn't understand the man's thick accent. "Can you say that again?"

"What are you doing here?" The guy spoke slower, but no louder. Bear's hunch that they were trying to keep a low profile seemed accurate.

Bear waved away the question like it was no big deal. "Taking a quick nap."

"You can't do that here."

"What?"

The man bit down hard, his lips thinning and his nostrils flaring. His voice was clear and he knew it. "You can't do that here."

"Why not?"

"This is a private settlement."

Bear looked around like he just realized where he was. "It is?"

"Sir, I need you to step out of the car."

"I don't know if I feel comfortable with that," Bear said. "I think I'm going to call the cops. We'll figure this out."

Bear reached into his pocket for a phone that wasn't there. The man reacted instantly, pulling his side piece and taking a step back from the car. He leveled the pistol at the window, but he wouldn't pull the trigger unless absolutely necessary.

Bear put his hands up. "What are you doing, man? I was just getting a couple hours of sleep. What's your problem?"

"Step out of the vehicle. I won't ask again."

Bear kept up the act as he pushed the door open and stood before the guy. It was clear the other man hadn't realized Bear's size until then. He took a step back and sized him up.

"What's the problem?" Bear asked. He kept his voice even. As confident as he was, the guy wasn't going to pull the trigger unless he had to, pushing his buttons wasn't a smart play.

The man held one hand to his ear as he listened to whoever was on the other end of his earpiece. Bear could just about make out the crackle of another voice in the silence of the night, but there was no way he could hear what was being said. He assumed they were checking in on him by running the plates on the suspicious-looking vehicle down the road.

Bear didn't understand the man's response, which was spoken in Chinese, low and quick. He did understand when the man looked up at him and said in English, "You're coming with me."

Bear planted his feet, his arms still in the air. "Where?"

"Now." The man moved behind Bear and poked him in the back with the barrel of his pistol. "Move."

Amateur move.

And all Bear needed.

He swung around, his elbow connecting with the man's wrist, knocking the gun from his hand. It clattered to the ground and under the Altima. The guard lunged for it. Bear was on top of him in a matter of seconds. He wrapped one arm around the man's neck and braced the back of his head with his other hand. Then he pulled and twisted until he felt a pop. The guard went limp in Bear's arms. His earpiece was still crackling with the annoyed voice of someone from inside the house.

"Guess that's my cue," Bear mumbled to himself.

Chapter Sixteen

B ear had sixty seconds at most to get to the front door of the house before they sent a scouting party for their missing guy. He grabbed the man's pistol from under the Altima, as well as his own 9mm. Anything bigger felt like overkill at this point, especially considering he didn't know how many innocent people were inside.

The street was dark enough for him to sprint from one shadow to the next without being seen. His goal was to get to the second floor, grab the package, and get out. After that he could dump the car and find another way to meet Cheung to deliver the goods.

Ideal?

No. But with any luck he'd remain a ghost and they'd be left with no way to track him down. He had enemies all over the world. A few more wouldn't hurt.

Bear chuckled to himself then muttered under his breath, "Famous last words."

He was kneeling at the corner of the porch, hidden from view, when he heard raised voices inside. Without waiting to consider if it was a good idea or not, Bear launched himself up and over the bannister and landed on the front porch with a slight thud. He took two giant steps forward and stood in front of the door. Before sense could get the best of him, he raised his leg and swung his foot out, planting it right above the handle. The door nearly came off the hinges as it swung inward. He got a snapshot of life inside the house before everything went to hell.

The man in the burgundy suit was sitting at the head of the table, a woman in his lap and two guards on either side. Four other men sat with him, playing cards and drinking. Looked like a print you could buy at one of the cheap stands outside the Met.

Everyone looked up when Bear walked through the door. One moment, all was still. He looked at them and they stared right back, faces frozen in shock or confusion. The next moment everyone was yelling and chairs were being knocked over and skidding across the room.

The man in the burgundy suit threw the woman off his lap and took off into the next room, his two bodyguards in tow. That left the four card players for Bear to deal with.

The man sitting closest to him on his right threw a solid glass ashtray at Bear's hand. It smacked just above the knuckle of his middle finger, causing his hand to flex open and knocking his 9mm to the ground.

The man on Bear's left jumped from his chair and swung it at Bear's head. It splintered into several pieces and knocked Bear off balance long enough for the man to grab the other gun and wrench it from Bear's hand. It clattered to the ground and slid under the table.

Bear felt panic rising in his throat at the fact that he had been disarmed so quickly, but when he looked around, he noticed none of the men had weapons in their hands or at their hips. They took flying under the radar seriously.

There was no time to collect his thoughts further than that.

The man who had thrown the ashtray kicked and knocked Bear down to one knee while the other attempted to pin his arm behind his back. Bear might have lost the advantage along with both his pistols, but he was by no means helpless. And he was at least twice as big as the rest of the men in the room.

With a grunt Bear wrenched his arm free from the second man and struck him in the chest with his other hand so hard the man's feet left the ground. The guy hit the floor and slid into the wall headfirst.

Bear leaned back and out of the way as the first man swung at him. Bear's hand landed on the ashtray, which was somehow still in one piece. He grabbed it and swung it as hard as he could at the first man's head. It shattered as blood erupted from the long gash in the man's forehead. The guy dropped to his knees and fell backward.

Bear got to his feet just as the remaining two men launched themselves at him. They looked like twins, and their moves mirrored each other in a way that could only happen if you trained with another person day in and day out. When one punched, the other kicked. It was a barrage of blows that forced Bear outside and onto the porch. He could feel bruises erupting on his forearms and legs as he tried to block as many hits as he could. He absorbed each blow and waited for his chance.

One of the brothers made the mistake of kicking too high. Bear let the hit land against his ribs, ignoring the pain long enough to grab the man's leg and twist it painfully out of the socket, eliciting a sharp scream. Bear didn't wait for the man to gain his where-withal. He picked him up and swung him around, tossing him through the bannister and into the front yard.

The other opponent didn't stop long enough to check whether his brother was still alive, but Bear could feel the anger in his furious blows. The coordination was gone from his attack. Bear gained control of the guy's dominant arm and then it was over.

He threw a haymaker at the other man's head that connected right at his temple. The second brother dropped and remained down.

Bear felt the effects of the fight, but it wasn't enough to stop him. He marched back through the door, expecting to be met with the next round of fighters.

Instead, he found an empty room except for the woman the man in the burgundy suit had thrown to the floor. She was still shaking and crying, covering her head with her hands and mumbling to herself.

There was something else missing from the room. The man Bear had punched in the chest had recovered and dragged his friend into the next room, taking Bear's pistols with him. So far they had tried to keep things quiet, but Bear wasn't about to let his guard down. A little bit of trouble with the neighbors would be worth it if it meant he made it out of this alive.

There was no doubt a stash of weapons was kept somewhere in the house, even if it was locked up to dissuade anyone from using them after a bad round of cards. Bear just had to make sure he got to them before the others did.

He crept low along one side of the table until he reached the woman on the floor. He waited between sobs before gently shaking her arm.

"How many more are in the house?"

The woman cried harder.

"Lady, I'm not going to hurt you. I just need to know how many more are in the house."

But it was no use. Her hysterics got loud enough that Bear backed away. He could handle four guys coming at him in a fight without a problem. But a crying woman? He found no shame in a quick retreat.

He kept to the wall as he snuck around the room toward the doorway. He had seen the man in burgundy run through there. A smeared blood trail led across the threshold. On the other side was a shiny black boot, heel up. A liability left to bleed out on the floor.

Whimpers came next room. The creak of a floorboard told him the group he was after had moved upstairs. There were at least four men left in the house, and who knows how many women. So far not a single gunshot had been fired. That wouldn't last long.

Bear leaned forward far enough to see into the next room and then straightened up again. His eyes took in the entire room in those few seconds. Two sofas, an armchair, a TV that was on but muted. Three women huddled behind the couch on the far side of the room, their wine glasses still half full on the coffee table. The man whose head Bear had bashed lay dead on the ground near the couch.

Bear took a step into the room, ignoring the gasps and cries from the women hiding on the other side. He searched the body of the dead man and came away with a switchblade. It wasn't much, but it was better than his fists alone.

He surveyed the room one last time to clear it, and then started to move up the stairs, keeping to the edges to make sure his approach was silent. He could hear muffled voices and the soft shuffle of feet above him, but he couldn't yet pinpoint their location. He had lost the element of surprise and they had gained the high ground. It had happened in such a short amount of time. Maybe he was slipping.

As soon as he hit the first landing, he heard the whir of a knife coming straight for his head. He ducked to the right before it landed with a thud and a wobble, buried up to the hilt in drywall. When he looked up, the man he had punched in the chest was standing at the top of the stairs, breathing heavily and bleeding from the side of his face.

Bear didn't hesitate. He yanked the knife out of the wall and drove himself upward. The other man only had time to turn and take a single step before Bear buried the knife in the back of his neck. He fell to his knees with a gurgle and a choke, then landed on his face. His body writhed for a few seconds then went still as blood soaked the carpet.

A door closed to the right. The man in the burgundy suit and his bodyguards.

Bear pulled the knife from the back of the dead man's neck and wiped it clean on the once-pristine suit. He tucked the switchblade in his pocket. The dead man's survival knife would make for a much better weapon. Bear still hadn't located his two guns. That was a problem. He presumed the bodyguards had a hold on them.

The hallway contained three doors. The first was open and led to the bathroom. Light beamed off the white floor. The other two doors were closed and neither had any light shining out from underneath the frame. Bear crept up to the first one and listened. Inside, three people were breathing heavily and whispering in another language.

Bear stood to the side and then reached over and knocked on the door. The whispers cut off, but no one fired a shot. That meant they were still on the defensive. Unless he had a knife to their boss's throat, they wouldn't aim a gun at him.

Bear squared up with the door and this time kicked it off its hinges. The room was filled with two couches and a bed, a small TV, and a wooden dresser. The man in the burgundy suit was crouched down behind the couch on the far side. One of his body-guards stood in front of him. The other was waiting for Bear as soon as he crossed the threshold.

The first bodyguard threw a punch that connected with Bear's jaw. A kick came next, but Bear had already regained his balance. He grabbed the man's leg and plunged the knife into his thigh. It was met with an angry scream. The bodyguard attempted to grab hold of Bear's head and plunge his thumb into his eye sockets, but Bear's knife was out of the guy's leg and inside his skull before any real damage could be done.

Bear heard the click of the hammer from the other end of the room and reacted instinctively. He moved the first bodyguard's body in between himself and the other men. Three shots were fired and Bear felt each one land center mass and he stalked across the room with his human shield. When he was nearly face to face with the last remaining bodyguard, Bear shoved the first man at him and sent them both to the ground. He didn't give the second man a chance to beg for his life before he retrieved his 9mm and put a bullet in the guy's head.

"And then there was one."

Bear turned to the man in the burgundy suit. When Bear had first spotted him walking up to the house, he thought the man was going to be the biggest badass of them all strutting around in his tailored suit and shiny shoes. But now he whimpered in the corner with his head tucked between his legs.

"Pathetic."

"Please," the man begged. "Please don't kill me."

"That's entirely up to you, man." Bear hauled the guy to his feet. The man swayed for a second before finding his balance. "What's your name?"

"W-Wong." There was snot running down his face. "My name is Wong."

"I've killed six of your men so far. Who else is here?"

"That's all of them," he stammered. "All the men I had with me."

"You're sure?" Bear pressed the barrel of the gun to Wong's neck. It was still hot. Not the smartest move, but this guy wouldn't do anything. Wong cried out as smoke rose from his skin. "You wouldn't happen to be lying to me, would you?"

"N-no. That was e-everyone. I swear. I swear!"

"Good man." Bear removed the barrel from Wong's neck. "I'm here to retrieve a package and I could use your help finding it."

Wong nodded his head emphatically. "Please, just don't kill me."

"Don't piss me off and you're free to live." Bear dragged Wong out into the hallway, then pointed at the last remaining door. "What's in there?"

"N-nothing." Wong seemed to think better of lying and before Bear could threaten him again, said, "Merchandise. That's it."

"Well, that happens to be where my package is. Northeast bedroom on the second floor." Bear pushed Wong ahead of him until they reached the end of the hallway. "Open the door."

Wong swallowed audibly but didn't hesitate. Bear was expecting him to wet himself at any moment. Instead, Wong retrieved a key and put a hand on the doorknob and turned it. The door creaked open wide.

Bear pushed Wong forward with the barrel of the gun. "Go on. Walk inside. I wanna make sure there are no surprises."

This time Wong did hesitate. At least until Bear moved the gun from the middle of his back to the back of his head. And then Wong marched right into the middle of the room.

Bear followed slowly. He heard a slight whimper, but he couldn't tell if it was Wong or someone else. The rest of the house was silent. He couldn't even hear the women crying downstairs anymore. He hoped they had gotten the hell out while they still could. Who knew if they would take the brunt of punishment for what had happened here tonight?

Bear walked up behind Wong and pushed him down to his knees. The other man automatically raised his arms in surrender, but Bear wasn't paying attention. The room was spartan except for what lay in the middle of it. When Bear had first walked in, Wong had been blocking his view. But he could see it clear as day now.

The package wasn't an envelope or a briefcase or a box.

It was a girl.

Chapter Seventeen

The young woman was curled up on the ground in the middle of the room. She was thin and ragged looking, her blonde hair covering her face like a greasy blanket. She wore a dress that must've been white at one point, but was now covered in blood and dirt. The sharp scent of her unwashed body attacked Bear's nose.

He gazed down at Wong, who was looking everywhere but at the girl. Bear's voice cut through the silence. "Who is she?"

"I-I don't know. I don't know her name."

Bear stepped around Wong, careful not to tread on the girl. When he was face to face with the man, he pointed the 9mm between the guy's eyes. "You said this room was full of merchandise."

"It's not me, I swear." Tears ran down Wong's face. "I have a boss. I'll tell you his name. I'll tell you anything you want to know."

"I warned you not to piss me off. You didn't keep up your end of the bargain."

Bear didn't bother waiting for Wong to come up with more

excuses. He pulled the trigger and sent Wong to hell with a single bullet. The ringing in his ears gave way to approaching sirens. The neighbors had finally caught on to the commotion happening in their cozy little community.

He brushed the girl's hair aside to look at her face. She was young, maybe still a teenager. Her eyes were open but glazed over. She was drooling out of one side of her mouth. Drugged.

"Are you injured?" Bear didn't expect a response, but if she could hear him, he wanted her to know that he was there to help. "I'm just going to check if anything is broken. I won't hurt you. Promise."

He waited another few seconds before reaching out and feeling each arm, each leg, and then the back of her head and down her spine. Other than a few bruises and light abrasions, she seemed fine, though he wasn't sure there weren't any internal issues he couldn't see. The drugs were keeping her numb enough that any pain wouldn't be bothering her now, but that didn't mean transporting her wouldn't cause additional issues down the line.

As the sirens grew louder he knew he couldn't stay any longer. And he wasn't about to leave her on her own, not knowing if the cops that found her were the kind that would help her. If what Cheung told him was true, this organization was well-connected, and that undoubtedly meant they had at least a handful of cops on their side.

Bear scooped the girl up in his arms, trying not to let her head flop around too much. She couldn't have weighed more than a hundred pounds, but she somehow felt even lighter than that.

Like she was hollow.

When was the last time she'd had a decent meal? How long ago had she been taken? Beyond the drugging, what had they done to her?

That same surge of white-hot anger that had caused him to pull the trigger on Wong washed over him. He wasn't just angry with the man who was now dead at his feet, but everyone who had led him to this moment, standing there with an unconscious girl in his arms. Had Cheung known what kind of package he had sent Bear to retrieve?

Had Thorne?

Bear took the stairs slowly, careful not to bump the girl on the wall or the railing on the way down. The first floor was deserted. The girls had run. Maybe they called the cops on the way out. Had they known what was upstairs? Were they part of the problem or were they just trying to avoid the same fate?

Walking out the front door was a death sentence. If the cops didn't catch him, he'd be spotted by the neighbors. Instead he headed through the back and into the kitchen. According to the blueprints Cheung had shown him, there was a back door that led to the next street over. Bear could circle around and hopefully be back in the rental car by the time the cops pulled up to the house.

He was halfway across the kitchen when he spotted an open laptop and a stack of file folders. Bear didn't know exactly what was going on with Wong and the girl and the organization at large, but he knew an operation when he saw one. She was just the tip of the iceberg, and he couldn't walk away in good conscience without uncovering what was under the surface.

He shifted the girl higher in his arms and snapped the laptop shut, grabbed the folders, and tucked both under his arm before kicking open the back door and walking out into the humid night air. The smell of the neighbor's dinner lingered in the alley. The sirens were closing in. Getting closer. Getting louder. Blue lights bouncing off the underside of tall trees.

After everything he'd gone through that night, the weight of the girl's small frame started to take its toll. Halfway down the block he stopped for a moment. He gently lowered her to the ground, tossed the laptop and files next to her, and stretched his arms, all while keeping his head on a swivel.

Ten seconds hadn't passed when the first cop car zipped by. It wasn't the typical black-and-white he was used to, but the sirens were a dead giveaway. The girl's white dress glowed in the dark despite how dirty it was. He'd avoided the pools of light cast down from the evenly spaced street lamps, but it might not matter. Anyone looking for someone in the shadows would be able to spot them.

Two more cop cars passed before there was a break. He could hear shouting coming from the direction of the house. Windows all around him lit up. Bear took that as his cue to run.

He scooped up the girl and the information he had retrieved from the house and gritted his teeth against the strain on his muscles. He avoided flat out sprinting. It might jostle her neck too much. But his pace was brisk enough that it only took a few more minutes before he was standing next to his car. Damn fine decision to move it to the other end of the street. He'd even had the forethought of turning the lights out so when he got back in the car, he wouldn't be spotted.

Bear pulled the back door open and laid the girl across the seat. He placed the computer and file folders on the floor near her. The door clicked shut and sounded like a rifle blast in the still air.

Bear opened his own door and slid behind the wheel. The engine sounded like it belonged to a fighter jet when it turned over. No one turned in his direction, but Bear wasn't going to take any chances. With one hand still holding his door shut, he put the car in drive and slowly pulled away from the curb, doing a quick U-turn to avoid having to drive past the house.

He was three streets over when he swung his door shut and turned on his lights. His eyes were glued to the rearview mirror, expecting the cops to flash their lights at any moment.

Chapter Eighteen

Bear made it out of the suburbs and back into the city with no issues, but that didn't mean his problems were over. He adjusted the rearview mirror to look at the girl in his back seat. She was still out of it, though there was no guarantee that was going to last much longer. All trips come to an end.

Worst yet, Bear didn't know where he could go. Did Cheung know that the package was actually a girl? Could he trust the guy enough to bring her back to him? The answers didn't come easily, and it was starting to make him antsy. What other options did he have? Cheung knew more than he did, and one way or another, Bear was going to make him talk.

It took close to an hour to get back to the park in downtown Hong Kong. Traffic wasn't the issue. Bear took as many circuitous routes as possible. As far as he could tell no one was following him. But real trouble didn't come when you knew you were being tailed. Real trouble came when you had no idea.

Still, the quicker he could get to Cheung the better.

A rustle of clothes from the backseat had Bear turning around to look down at the girl he'd rescued from the house. She blinked against the lights and shielded her eyes with her hand. Her dazed eyes danced around. When she spotted Bear her eyes grew wide and she tried to push as far away from him as possible. But there was only so far you could go in the back of an Altima.

"Wait, wait, wait." Bear was twisted awkwardly in his seat and he held up both hands. "I'm not gonna hurt you."

"Who the hell are you?" She choked back a sob. "Where the hell are we? What the fuck is going on?"

"Bear."

The girl stopped and looked up at him. "Bear?"

"Yeah."

Her pupils were shrinking to a normal size. "And where's this? Where are we?"

"A parking lot." He pointed to the park adjacent to the lot. "A park in Hong Kong."

She sat up and placed her forearm on the passenger seat, leaned into it. Her gaze drifted to the marks on her arm and she grimaced. "How'd I get here?"

Bear bit back the urge to scrunch his face up at the fresh wave of body odor. "I got you out of that house. Brought you here."

"Are you with the CIA or something?"

Quite a leap for her to ask him that. Who was she expecting?

"Not quite." He paused, unsure how much to tell her. Not sure how much she could handle. "What's your name?"

"Maria." She pressed harder against the seat back but it did little to stop her from shaking. The car bounced a little in response. "Maria Thompson."

"You remember anything?"

She closed her eyes, squeezing a tear out of the corner, and shook her head. "One minute I was walking down the street to meet a friend, and the next I was in the back of a van with a needle in my arm surrounded by three people with black ski masks.

Everything after that is spotty. Blurry. I remember glimpses... Flashes of moments here and there. But it's like a puzzle where too many pieces are missing and the ones that remain don't line up."

A laugh from outside the car jostled them both. Maria lurched backward and hit her head on the ceiling. The dome light switched on.

Bear reached up and turned it off. "It's okay. You're safe with me."

I hope.

Maria's head swung violently side to side as sobs escaped her. A fresh sheen of sweat beaded up along her forehead and chest. "I can't be here. They're gonna find me. I gotta go."

She tried the handle, but the child lock was activated. Her stare cut Bear. She looked up at him as though he'd betrayed her.

Like *he* had been the one who had been keeping her prisoner.

"You stay with me. I gotta keep you safe."

"I'm not safe!" Maria's voice hit a frenzied pitch. "They've got people everywhere. Spies everywhere. They'll find me and once they know where I am, they'll kill me. Please, you have to let me go."

How much did she know?

"What did they drug you with?"

She looked down at her arm, at the track marks. Yellow bruises surrounded the oldest ones. She shook her head. Bear found himself doing the same.

"How long've they drugged you? Days? Weeks?"

"I don't know. Don't you get that?" She pushed hard into the seat and bit down on her finger while her body shook even harder.

"All right, look. You can get out. I'll let you go. But withdrawal is kicking in already."

She turned toward the window and hid her face.

"You wanna do that alone?" he said. "Or with me there to help you through?"

"What do you know about it?"

"Enough."

"I can take care of myself." She tried to sound defiant, but there was still a wobble in her voice.

"I don't doubt it. But it's an enemy no one can battle. I mean, what're you gonna do? Sleep next to a gutter while you're puking your brains out?"

Maria pushed a greasy chunk of blond hair out of her eyes and looked out the window, still squinting against the sun. She didn't say anything, but a subtle nod of her head was enough to tell Bear he had won her over. For now at least.

"I'm supposed to be meeting someone here," Bear said. "Someone who's supposedly helping me. He led me to you and I think we can trust him."

She looked as unconvinced as he felt. "You think?"

"I can count the number of people I trust on one hand. He's not one of them." Bear aimed the vent at his face and took a deep breath. "We don't have a choice."

She bit her bottom lip and gave a slight nod.

"He wanted to meet in the park. That's out. You can't be out there."

"I can stay in—"

"No." He sliced his hand through the air, causing her to flinch. "I'm not gonna leave your side."

Maria wiped a layer of sweat off her forehead. Her voice sounded weaker than it did even a minute or two ago. "So what's the plan?"

He held up his phone. "Let's see if he's got a better idea."

Bear twisted back around in his seat and stared down at his phone. This was a bad idea. He knew it. There was no trust in Cheung. What other options did he have? Against his better judgement and his instincts he dialed Thorne's contact and waited as the line rang.

But all his worry was for nothing. The line rang a dozen times and then cut off without so much as a voicemail message. Bear checked the connection. He had full service and plenty of battery life. He redialed. Same thing. A dozen rings. A click. Then nothing.

A slight chill ran down his spine. Could they track him from the call?

"What's wrong?" Maria's voice grew quieter with every sentence. Her knee jammed against his seat. Felt like a vibrating chair.

"No answer." Bear scanned his surroundings but didn't see anything out of place.

"They're gonna find me out here." Maria drew her knees to her chest. "They're gonna find me."

"All right." Bear put both hands on the steering wheel and gripped it until his knuckles turned white. This wasn't a situation he felt comfortable improvising. Too many things could go wrong. Too few friends to bail him out. "All right, we're gonna get out of here. Head someplace safer."

"Nowhere is safe." She hugged her knees tight and rocked back and forth. "They got him and they're gonna get me too."

Bear threw the car in reverse and jammed his foot down on the accelerator. A couple walking hand in hand jumped from his path. Paranoia was setting in and it was only gonna get worse from here on out. For both of them.

He needed to find somewhere they could lay low for a day or two where no one would ask questions. Somewhere Maria could ride out the storm of withdrawal in peace.

Somewhere Bear could finally get some goddamn answers.

Chapter Nineteen

Paranoia is contagious. This fact is lost on most people. Not Bear. He knew. He felt it. He became drenched with it. The more Maria mumbled about how they were going to find her and kill her, the more Bear looked over his shoulder. He only made it a couple blocks before he pulled over and ditched his burner phone. Then he drove another few minutes and stopped to pick up two more just in case. He was mindful of the cameras on the street and in the store, never giving them a good angle.

He half-expected Maria to be gone by the time he made it back to the car, but she was still there. Sweat glistened her heaving body. It soaked through her clothing. Looked like she'd dove into the ocean. She looked paler than she had an hour ago, and her hair more disheveled and soaked in perspiration.

He called a taxi from inside the car and waited in silence with Maria until the driver pulled up alongside them. If the man thought it was strange they were getting out of a perfectly good car to get into his vehicle, he didn't say anything. Take the money and ask no questions. Bear said it. The guy obliged.

Maria's condition worsened by the minute. She looked half-dead. There was nothing he could do to help her blend in. He gave her his jacket. It was at least four sizes too big for her, but it did the job of hiding her stained clothing. He realized for the first time that she wasn't wearing any shoes as she walked across the narrow stretch of asphalt and slipped into the back of the taxi. Nothing he could do about that now.

Bear instructed the driver to take them to the outskirts of Hong Kong Island. When they reached the area, he picked a corner at random and handed the driver a wad of bills. The man sped off without a word. Bear hoped he wouldn't remember their faces. But that was unlikely. It wasn't so much they were two Americans in the middle of Hong Kong. They were two very distinct Americans in Hong Kong. Between Bear's hulking frame and Maria's zombie-like condition, they were bound to leave an impression.

That was the least of his worries. He looked down at Maria. She stared at the pavement beneath her feet. Sweat dripped from her nose and splashed between her big toes.

"Are you okay to walk?"

She looked up at him. She had bright blue eyes the size of quarters. Red scratched like lightning in the whites of her eyes. She was attractive beneath all the sweat and dirt. Her frame was thin but lean like an athlete's. She seemed sharp too. Despite her condition, her gaze rarely remained still after he snapped her out of the trance. She scanned the street. Somehow Bear didn't think it was just the paranoia. It was a habit.

As he stared into her eyes he wondered again who she was and where she had come from.

He adjusted the duffle bag on his shoulder and put a gentle hand on her back. She jumped but then leaned into it, like she was grateful for the extra support.

"We need to walk," Bear said. "I'm not sure for how long. Until we find a motel that won't ask questions."

Maria nodded and put one foot in front of the other. Bear kept pace, his hand still against her back. If she slowed, he nudged her forward. If she sped up, he grasped the fabric and pulled her back. The streets were sparse. The few people they passed didn't bother looking in their direction. That was a plus about being in the city. Everyone was too busy to be in your business. That meant even fewer people who'd remember their faces.

He didn't know anything about this part of Hong Kong, but he knew this kind of area. A little darker, a little seedier, a little more dangerous.

He was less worried about getting jumped and more concerned that Maria would collapse before they could find accommodations for the night. The last thing he wanted to do was heave her over his shoulder and ask for a room.

"Bear." Maria's voice sounded like the desert, cracked with dryness and pain. "I'm not feeling so hot."

"I know." He gripped her lower back, encouraging her to walk a little faster. "Couple more minutes."

"I'm gonna throw up."

He glanced around for an alley to duck into. Nothing looked promising. "Hold it down."

Maria squeezed her eyes shut. She reached back and put her hand over his. Her palms were slick and hot.

In the distance he spotted a cheap hotel among the signs. The kind of place they needed. He picked up speed, but Maria stumbled. It would've been faster to carry her but also a lot more suspicious. He made do with her pace, as slow as it was. It wouldn't do either of them good if he pushed her too hard right before the finish line.

Would bringing her inside draw too much attention? Should he leave her outside while he grabbed a room? He contemplated it for a moment. He didn't trust her not to wander off in a state of paranoia. And he certainly didn't trust this neighborhood to leave a wandering American woman alone. She could barely stand, let alone fight off any attackers.

They walked through the front door and were hit with the smell of a meal. His stomach knotted in response.

He made eye contact with the old woman who ran the motel. He was expecting to see the trepidation in her eyes. She didn't disappoint.

"One room, one night," he said.

The woman looked between him and the girl and then shook her head.

"It's not like that." This *was* the kind of place where things like that happened. The old lady was used to seeing men walk in here with women in various states of disorder all the time. She wouldn't say anything, even when she should. So long as the man dropped a few extra bills on the counter like Bear had.

The woman didn't respond. She tapped a few things into her computer and printed out an invoice. Bear tapped the stack of bills and scooped up the room key.

He looked into the room behind the counter and spotted a plate of noodles on a circular wooden table.

"Any chance—"

But the woman dodged him and closed the door.

A minute later they found the room. It was small with a single bed covered with a green blanket. An overstuffed chair was placed in the corner. Wasn't much, but it would be enough for them for the night. He found it relatively clean and somewhat off the beaten track. The latter was most important. They couldn't stay here for long, but it would be enough to get Maria through the worst of it.

Maria didn't pause long enough to take the room in. She headed for the bathroom and slammed the door behind her. The thin walls did little to hide the heaving and wrenching sounds. He turned the TV on to give her some semblance of privacy. A game show that involved seven people climbing a greased plastic slide to reach a barrel full of cash was playing.

Bear tossed his bag on the bed and pulled out the laptop and the file folders. It would be a long night, might as well take advantage of it.

A n hour into his deep dive, Maria emerged from the bathroom. He'd checked on her every ten minutes. She looked exhausted and weak, but her gaze was sharper. He felt like she was taking him in when she looked at him. He had taken up residence in the uncomfortable chair on the other side of the bed, and it was obvious she was grateful that he had left the mattress all for her.

"Here." He passed her one of the several bottles of water he had slipped out of the room to get. "You need to drink as much as you can keep down."

She grabbed the bottle without a word and sipped it gingerly.

"Your abs hurt?"

She nodded and winced. "Every goddamn pore in my skin hurts."

"Finish that bottle and get some rest. Got a feeling it's not over yet."

She tried for a wry laugh, but it came out as a cough. She doubled over in pain. She took another sip of water. "What are you working on?"

Bear held up one of the folders. "Figuring out what was going on in that house and why they had you there."

Maria stiffened but managed to keep her voice steady. "Learn anything yet?"

"More than I wanted to." He said his next words slowly. "You said you only remember flashes."

"Glimpses here and there, yeah." She took another sip of water. "It's all a blur. They kept me drugged most of the time."

Bear sighed and leaned forward. "I can't help you unless I know what's going on."

"I told you, I—"

"Don't remember anything, yeah." Bear ran a hand down his face. "Thing is, I'm not sure I believe you."

Maria's gaze flickered to the door and back, though she didn't move a muscle.

Bear leaned back in his chair. "I'm not gonna hurt you. I'm not gonna keep you against your will. Once you're on your feet, you're free to leave. But I do want to know what's going on here." He tapped his finger against the folder. "If I can do something about it, I will."

"So you're one of those, aren't you?"

"One of what?"

"The good guys."

Bear laughed. "There's no such thing. And there's plenty of people who'd disagree with you."

"And I bet there are a lot of people out there who wouldn't. And there is such a thing." Maria watched as Bear shrugged. She looked down at her hands for a moment, and when she looked up again, there was determination in her eyes. "I don't remember much."

"Anything you know can help." Bear held up the folders. "I've got a whole pile of nonsense here. Most of it is written in short-hand and I can only make out half. Lots of rosters and shipment details. Far as I can tell, they're trafficking young girls across the globe. The bids are high, which makes me think they're going to some pretty wealthy people."

Maria's voice was small when she spoke. "They liked Americans the best. Blondes, like me." She flinched as she ran her hand through her matted hair. "I don't know why. Exotic, maybe? Different? But I was with a bunch of other girls. Maybe twenty altogether. They separated us pretty early on, but I still remember some of their faces."

Maria folded her arms across her stomach and began sobbing. Bear wanted to comfort her, but he didn't move. The last thing she needed was another man to touch her, even if it was to help.

"These guys who grabbed you… Did you recognize them? Do you know who they were? Who they worked for?"

She shook her head, her cries coming in waves now. She kept apologizing, and Bear kept trying to reassure her. But it was no use. She was getting herself worked up. She leaned over to the side of the bed and threw up. Nothing but water and a little phlegm came out, but it was obvious the effort had drained her of nearly all her strength.

"All right, we'll talk later."

Bear made Maria take another sip of her water before he set the bottle on the nightstand. Then he helped her under the covers and told her to sleep. She was still shaking, and he was sure she'd throw up a few more times before the night was over. There was nothing they could do but ride it out.

He sat back into the overstuffed chair and opened up the laptop. He wasn't surprised to find that it was locked, but a glimmer of hope had existed that the thugs he took it from might've been too stupid to put a password to it. No such luck.

Bear drummed his fingers on the armrest and stared up at the ceiling. It had water damage in one corner and what looked like dried blood in the opposite. They couldn't stay in the place for too long, but he also didn't know where he could go.

He considered calling Jack again, but he already knew that number was out of commission. Besides, if Thorne tracked him last time he'd tried calling Noble, chances were someone else would too.

Thinking of Thorne led Bear to think of Sadie. How were the two connected? Had Thorne gotten Sadie mixed up in this mess too? Sadie had wanted to take it easy after Costa Rica. Wanted being a loose term. She was being brought in. She was an adventurous woman who wouldn't be content with run-of-the-mill jobs for long.

Had Thorne reached out to her and promised her a more exciting mission? Sadie was smart enough to stay away from him, but Thorne was also smart enough to pull on her heartstrings. That's how Bear ended up here, after all. The guy had a knack for it.

Maybe he was one of the good guys.

He resisted the urge to call Thorne. Talking to him now would only allow him to spin the facts in his favor. It was better if Bear could look through the laptop first and then reach out. Maybe he'd be able to catch the man in a lie. That would be more revealing than anything Thorne could come up with on his own.

But that still left him the problem of the laptop. He didn't know anyone in Hong Kong well enough to trust them with the information that potentially resided on the device, especially if Maria was along for the ride.

He wracked his brain and landed on the name of someone he hadn't seen in quite some time: Ernest Neumann.

They hadn't spoken in years, not since his early days in the program. But Neumann was trustworthy. Better yet, he was close. He'd retired to the Philippines a few years ago. As far as Bear knew, the guy was still there.

Now Bear just had to hope that Neumann was willing to get himself mixed up in whatever Bear was slowly uncovering.

Chapter Twenty

I t took several calls and multiple burner phones, but Bear finally tracked down a number for Ernest Neumann. His old buddy wasn't too happy about being found after all these years, but he was a good soul and couldn't resist helping a friend.

Especially after Bear told him what he had potentially uncovered.

And it seemed the universe was throwing them a bone. Neumann was already in Hong Kong on some business with the government. He was packing up to leave when Bear reached out to him and was willing to delay his departure by an hour so they could meet him at the docks.

Maria felt better in the morning but still weak and nauseous. The worst had passed though. She insisted on showering before they left, and Bear didn't disagree. It zapped her of her remaining strength. When Bear went to rinse off he found the hot water used up. Didn't matter. A cold shower would bring on his third wind. Afterward he called a taxi and paid the man extra to get them to the docks in record time.

Neumann was just tossing the mooring lines back onto the boat when Bear stepped foot on the dock. He looked older than Bear remembered, but it had been close to seven years since he had seen him last. In that amount of time, his salt and pepper hair had turned completely gray and he had grown a thick mustache that covered his upper and lower lips.

"Well, look who finally decided to show up." Neumann reached over and shook Bear's hand. Then he turned his attention to Maria. "This her?"

"No, she's arriving via chopper. This is her body double."

Neumann rolled his eyes and reached his hand out. "Maria, I presume." He helped her step up onto the boat deck. "Come on, dear. The sea's a rockin' today. Won't be too kind to you. I've got a good bed and a big bucket waiting for you downstairs."

Maria cracked a smile. Bear could tell it was forced. "Thanks."

Neumann led her below deck while Bear boarded. The boat was older, but well taken care of. The paint was a little faded, but she still shone in the sunlight. Neumann was of a different generation. He pinched a penny—even when he didn't have to. Bear respected him for that. Among other things.

When Neumann emerged from down below his face betrayed his concern. "Surprised she's walking."

"Tough girl." Bear watched as Neumann raised the anchor and got ready to push off. "I don't envy her."

"Me neither. If she's been drugged for weeks her symptoms aren't going to go away any time soon. And these waters aren't exactly smooth sailing."

Bear stepped up next to Neumann while he navigated out of the port. "How'd you end up getting a free pass to sail across the open ocean between Hong Kong and the Philippines?"

"I do some odd jobs for the government here and there."

"Thought you were retired?"

"I am retired." Neumann glared side-eyed. "But I still gotta make money."

Bear chose his next words carefully. "And all of this is…"

"On the books. C'mon, man. You know me. You really have to ask?"

Bear held up his hands in surrender. "People change. It's been a while. Making sure, is all."

Neumann pressed a couple buttons and turned around, arms folded across his chest. "Besides, shouldn't I be the one worrying about you?"

"Me?"

"I may not have kept tabs on you, but I've heard murmurings through the grapevine."

Bear shifted from one leg to the other. He had always considered Neumann more of a friend than a father figure, but the reprimand was clear, even if it wasn't verbal. "I do what I gotta do."

"I know." Neumann's voice was even. "The girl is evidence of that. But you didn't reach out to hear me lecture you."

"As much fun as that would be—" Bear opened the duffle bag and pulled out the laptop, "—I need your help with this."

Neumann set them up in the kitchen below deck. The smell of brewing coffee filled the air. After a quick breakfast sandwich and a healthy dose of java, he cleared off the table and set up his equipment. It didn't take much to crack the laptop with his gadgets. The system wasn't military-grade or anything near that caliber. It was just a run-of-the-mill computer with a simple password. No match for the guy. He broke through in a matter of minutes and then lit a thick cigar. Bear declined when offered.

Neumann hovered his hands over the keyboard and looked up at Bear. "All right. What're we looking for?"

Bear pulled out the file folders, waved the smoke out of his face with them, and then opened to the first sheet of paper. "Anything to do with shipments like these. This is full of rosters and schedules, but it's all in shorthand and code. I'm hoping the real documents are on there."

"Got it. Go sit over there. Can't concentrate when you're hovering. I'll call you over when I've got a full picture."

Bear couldn't stand the idea of doing nothing. The only reason he complied was because his body was starting to give up on him. Lack of sleep and all the adrenaline that had been running through his veins in the last couple days had left him exhausted. A few days ago he had been locked up in jail on St. Lucia. A few weeks before that? Living the life in paradise.

It felt like a lifetime ago.

He'd shut his eyes when he heard Neumann calling his name.

"Rise and shine, Sleeping Beauty. I've got answers."

Bear rubbed the sleep from his eyes. "How long was I out?"

"Three hours," Neumann said, his bushy mustache twitching as he smiled. "You look like you need about thirty more. Ain't gonna get them today. Come check this out."

Bear rose to his feet with a groan, rubbing the back of his neck and trying to loosen up the muscles. The chair was shit for sleeping. Most were.

"How's Maria doing?"

"Heard her puking her brains out about an hour ago. Checked on her after that and she was asleep. Sweaty and pale, but she drank about two bottles of water. She'll ride it out. Us too I suppose"

"Easier said than done."

Neumann shrugged. "She looks tough. Besides, she doesn't have an alternative. Would've been better to wean her off, but that's not really an option."

"Not even sure what they were using." Bear circled the table and came to stand behind Neumann. The laptop screen was full of tabs and pictures and text boxes. He couldn't make heads nor tails of it. "What am I looking at?"

Neumann sighed. There was a weight to it that made the hair on the back of Bear's neck stand on end. "It's not good."

"I had a feeling. Sex trafficking?"

"One of the biggest operations I've ever seen." Neumann clicked around until he brought up a satellite image of a house. "I started off easy. Didn't even bother going through the computer's documents before I knew what I was looking for."

"That's the house where I found her." Bear pointed toward the screen.

"I Googled the address." Neumann laughed, but it was hollow. "Amazing what you can find on the internet these days. Remember when we had to work for this shit?" His smile faded as his gaze drifted back to the screen. "Anyway, I found the owner of the house."

"Who is it?"

Neumann switched tabs and a picture of a man Bear had never seen popped up. "Joon Yi. On paper, he's just another businessman living in Hong Kong. Deals in real estate. High rises. Commercial. Some housing complexes. This house is marked down as a business expense. They use it as a meeting room when they want to get out of the city."

"It looked more like a pleasure house," Bear said.

"It's surprisingly easy to get away with shit like that, especially when you have as much money as Joon Yi. But that's not even the most interesting part." Neumann tapped the screen with the tip of his finger. "Our friend here is Korean. From the North."

"Now I'm paying attention."

Neumann smoothed his mustache before continuing. "His story is a little too squeaky clean. Basically boils down to him becoming a rising leader in North Korea and being granted leave to Hong Kong to continue to grow his business. He's doing a pretty good job of it too. In the last few years profits have continued to grow at an astronomical rate."

The boat rocked to the side and Bear had to grip the table to stay upright. He waited to speak until he was sure they weren't going to capsize. "Coercion?"

"Likely. But it's still a legitimate business as far as I can tell. You can solve a lot of problems with money."

"And those that can't be solved with money can be solved with intimidation." Bear watched as Neumann scrolled through the website, including a page on all of Joon Yi's employees. "Wait. There. Go back."

Neumann scrolled back up the page until he landed on a face Bear knew all too well.

"The man in the burgundy suit," Bear said. "He was at the house that night."

Maria appeared in the doorway, holding tight to the frame to remain upright. "His name was Seung Kim."

"You shouldn't be on your feet." Bear hurried toward her.

Maria held up her hand. "There's something I have to tell you. I was supposed to be there, at that house. But things didn't go the way I planned them. I failed my mission."

Bear's arms dropped back to his side. He felt his gut tighten. "Your mission?"

"My mission was Seung Kim." She grimaced as she swallowed. "I was there to kill him."

Chapter Twenty-One

For a solid minute all Bear could hear were the waves crashing against the stern. His ears rang with Maria's words. His entire perception of the girl had just been flipped on its head leaving him blindsided and dizzy.

"How old are you?" He didn't know why this was the first question he decided to ask, but in that moment it seemed important.

"Twenty." Maria tried for a smile, but it looked more like a grimace. "I look younger, right? That was sort of the point. Most of the girls there were younger than me. A lot younger."

Bear's thoughts settled as the reality of the situation set in. There was nothing to turn back to. They could only move forward. "Who are you?"

Maria made her way over to a chair and sat down with a groan. "My name is Maria Thompson. I didn't lie to you, Bear. I just left out a few details."

"Some pretty important details. Who do you work for?"

The hesitation was obvious. If Bear were in her position, he wouldn't want to betray his superiors either. But she was in deep now, and he and Neumann were trying to help her out of it. The trust had already been earned.

"A man named Thorne."

There was a beat of silence before Bear threw his head back and laughed. It was long and loud and bordered on hysteria. By the time he finished, there were tears in his eyes. He swiped them away and chuckled one more time. All he wanted to do was sleep and pretend Thorne didn't exist.

"I think I'm missing the joke," Neumann said. "Who's Thorne?"

"A pain in my ass." Bear made his way over to the couch and flopped onto it. "And the reason why I'm in the middle of this shitstorm."

"That sounds like him," Maria said. There was no humor in her voice.

Bear turned to her. "How do you know him?"

"I was what you called a *troubled youth*. In and out of juvie. Mostly for breaking and entering, stealing. I wasn't afraid to experiment with drugs. Landed in the hospital a couple times. But I was smart. I knew how to play the pity card. Never got into any real trouble. Moved around enough that no one really caught on to my longest con, which was pretending I was a lot more remorseful than I was."

Maria took a couple sips of her water before she continued. "I don't know how he found me. One day he just showed up. I was seventeen and he offered me a new life. Money, power, and best yet, the ability to truly take care of myself. He trained me to keep up the good girl appearances. Between my age and my looks, I was always underestimated. He and I ran small cons for about a year before he started using me for bigger operations."

"So you became a spy? At eighteen?" Bear had heard stories like this, but he'd never met anyone who had lived that life. He didn't envy her.

Maria shrugged. She looked sad. "A spy. A killer."

Neumann's voice was quiet. "That's no life for someone as young as you."

A flash of anger crossed Maria's face. "It's a better life than I had before. At least now I know where my next meal is coming from."

"But something went wrong here," Bear prodded. As much as he wanted to save Maria from Thorne's grasp, she was an adult. She had made her choice. The best he could hope for was that she'd make a new one by the end of all this.

"I was there to assassinate Seung Kim. I don't know why. Didn't ask. Not my place." She swallowed and winced but continued. "I allowed myself to be taken by the people who ran the house. According to Thorne, I was exactly his type. But I hadn't counted on the drugs taking hold so strongly. When the time came, he chose me, but I was too powerless to do anything. There are a few hazy days in between there and the house where you found me. Don't really remember much else."

"Do you know a woman named Sadie?" Bear asked.

Maria shook her head. Bear got up and took over the computer from Neumann. He pulled up a picture of Sadie and spun the laptop toward the girl.

"Never saw her," Maria said.

"So she never made it to the house?"

"I only saw a few faces here and there. They kept most of us apart." Maria clutched her stomach and waited for the nausea to pass before speaking again.

Neumann pointed at the picture of Sadie. "Was she an assassin?"

"No, but she trained to get close to male targets. She's one of the best. If she's involved in this, I don't think she'd be going after someone like Seung Kim. Her target would be someone like Joon Yi."

"Or someone bigger." Maria looked up at the two men. "Someone even more important than him."

Bear moved around the table again to stand in front of her. "What do you know?"

Maria's gaze flicked back to the picture of Sadie. "She's older, right? Older than me."

Bear nodded. "Why?"

Maria leaned back in her chair and closed her eyes. Bear could see the wheels turning, so he didn't interrupt her, though he had an urge to shake the information out of her. He felt like Sadie was so close, even if he had no idea where she was. This was the kind of mission she had been trained for. If she was mixed up in this at all, it would be here. And right now Maria was their best chance at finding Sadie.

"Thorne told me there was another job going down at the same time as mine. It had to do with taking out a North Korean general. Someone very important. But he told me to steer clear. Said it was too big for me." She opened her eyes, a wry smile on her face. "I was a brat. I tried arguing with him. Told him I could handle it. But he said it wouldn't work. I wasn't his type. I'm guessing now that I might've been too young for him."

Bear looked back at the picture of Sadie. She wasn't old by any definition of the word, but it sounded like this sex trafficking ring wasn't all that interested in women above the legal age limit. If the general wanted someone older and a little more experienced, however, they would absolutely accommodate him, especially if he was as powerful as Maria made him out to be.

"Do you know his name?" Neumann asked. "See what I can find."

Maria nodded. "It was the only thing I could find out about him before Thorne caught me. General Pyeong."

"If he's as big of a deal as you make him sound, we shouldn't have any trouble finding some basic information about him."

"There's another problem," Bear said, looking past Neumann and out the window behind him, where he had spotted another boat approaching. "We've got company."

Chapter Twenty-Two

Neumann slammed the laptop shut and shoved it and the file folders into Bear's arms as he ran past them and up the stairs. "There's a small compartment hidden behind the head of the bed in the other room. Hide in there until I tell you the coast is clear."

Bear barely had time to catch all the words before Neumann was gone. He handed Maria the laptop and folders and steered her toward the bedroom next door. When he pulled the bed about a foot out from the wall, he found a panel that slid to the right and a compartment that looked like it couldn't even hold Maria, let alone both of them.

"It's gonna be tight." Bear helped Maria slip inside. "I'll be back in a minute."

There was panic in her eyes. "But he told you to stay here with me."

Bear slid the compartment door about halfway shut. "I'm gonna see if I can figure out who's on our tail. I'll be right back."

Maria nodded, though she looked unconvinced, and sat back,

hugging her knees to her chest. Bear closed the door the rest of the way and moved the bed back into place. Then he turned around and sprinted back upstairs.

It was well past midnight, but the foreign boat's lights were bright enough that you couldn't miss them. They weren't bothering to approach stealthily. They wanted to be spotted.

Neumann turned around as soon as he heard Bear enter the wheelhouse. "I told you to hide."

Bear shrugged casually as he peered out the front window at the approaching vessel. "Never was a good listener."

"At least some things haven't changed." Neumann returned to the wheel. "I tried hailing them with no answer."

"So they wanted to be spotted, but they don't want us to know who they are just yet."

"They'll have more advantage that way." Neumann leaned forward to get a better look. "They might try to convince us they're the coast guard."

"How do you know they're not?" Bear asked.

"I know just about everyone worth knowing on the marine police force around here. I have clearance to sail. They don't bother me. This isn't them."

There was a streak of red across the sky as the other boat fired a flare that flew right over their heads. Bear watched as it arced and then landed some thirty yards or so past them.

"Well they're not trying to hit us," Bear said.

"But they're definitely trying to send us a warning." Neumann looked Bear dead in the eye. "I need you to go downstairs now. Hide. It'll be worse if they find you here. If I'm sailing by myself, they'll have no reason to give me trouble."

"They'll want to search the boat. If they find us, they might kill you."

"It's part of the job. You think I haven't done this before? I may be retired, but the job is never over. Haven't lost anyone yet. Need you to trust me."

Bear opened his mouth to ask about a hundred different questions. What was Neumann up to in his spare time? Smuggling refugees out of the country? Rescuing prisoners of war? He hadn't even considered the idea that Neumann might still be working under the radar and that made Bear speechless.

But now was not the time to catch up with his old friend. He slapped Neumann on the back and wished him good luck, then sprinted back downstairs and slipped into the bedroom. He felt Neumann rev the engines and start moving at a considerable speed. Maybe they'd be able to outrun the other vessel.

When he reached the bed, Bear called out to Maria so he wouldn't startle her.

He heard a muffled response before he pulled the bed back and then slid the panel open. Maria looked worried, but relatively calm. She had moved to the other side of the tiny compartment in order to let Bear crawl in easier. But there was nothing easy about it. After several grunts and a few choice curses, he managed to squeeze himself inside. They were sitting knee to knee and it was anything but comfortable.

"Can you close the panel?" she asked.

Bear's elbow was sticking several inches out of the compartment. "I don't think so."

Instead he grabbed the side of the bed and pulled it closer. It wouldn't do them much good if someone was really looking for them. But he'd have a better chance at hearing what was going on upstairs if the other boat somehow managed to catch up to them.

"Who are they?" Maria whispered.

"Not sure." Bear tried shifting to get comfortable, but it just managed to make Maria hiss in pain.

"But they're after me."

Bear looked over at her. In the darkness, he could only really see the shine of her blond hair and the whiteness of her teeth. "More than likely."

"I'm sorry I got you mixed up in all this."

"We can both blame Thorne for that," Bear said. His voice turned gruffer on the man's name. "He's the one who orchestrated all this. The one pulling the strings."

"Still, I..."

Maria cut off but Bear didn't need to ask her why. The boat slowed down. After a few minutes, it nearly came to a stop. The slower it went the rougher it felt.

"What's going on?" she whispered.

"Couldn't outrun them." Bear shifted again, this time managing to avoid hurting Maria. "Neumann's gonna try to negotiate with them now."

"Negotiate?" There was a tremor in her voice.

He looked over at her. "He's not going to give us up."

"How sure are you about that?"

"Very." He leaned to the side, straining his hearing to see if he could make out what was going on above deck. "You might think I'm a good guy, but I *know* Neumann is. He'd rather die than turn us over."

"You'd let it get that far?"

Bear didn't hesitate. "Not a chance."

They quieted at the sound of muffled footsteps from above. Sounded like Neumann had stepped out of the wheelhouse and was waiting on deck to speak to the passengers of the other boat.

A few silent minutes ticked by. Bear could feel their collective heartbeats in that tiny room. He tried not to notice how close the walls were around him. He hoped Maria wasn't claustrophobic.

He could just about make out Neumann's words above. "Sorry about the runaround. Thought you guys might be pirates. Didn't notice your colors until you got a bit closer. What can I do for you gentlemen?"

Bear heard shouting in another language, though he couldn't quite make it out. Then several pairs of boots hit the deck. Neumann's voice got louder, but Bear couldn't tell if it was because he was closer or if he had decided to start yelling.

"Whoa, whoa, whoa. You don't board a man's home without permission and expect to be treated with hospitality."

More yelling in a foreign language.

"I'm not understanding a word you're saying. Anyone speak English here?"

There was a beat of silence. Another pair of boots hit the deck. A new voice was added to the fray. "Where is she?"

"Where's who?" Neumann asked.

"The girl!" The other man's voice was thickly accented, but Bear could still make it out. He was louder than all the others. "Where is the girl?"

"I don't know what girl you're talking about," Neumann said. "I'm by myself here. There's no one else on the ship."

"You're lying."

There was another beat of silence, and then Neumann's voice grew even louder. "Hey, hey, hey. There's no need for that. We're having a civilized conversation here."

"We will kill you," the man said, "without hesitation. Unless you tell us where the girl is."

That was Bear's cue. He shifted the bed away from the opening to the compartment and started crawling out.

Maria put her hand on his arm and kept him in place. "What are you doing?"

"I won't let him die for us. There's only a couple of them. Even if they think someone else is on board, they're going to expect you, not me."

Maria's face drew tight. "Don't leave me."

If she were in better condition, the two of them could take out their pursuers without any trouble. But she was too sick and too weak to do anything but stay hidden. So he slid the panel closed, pushed the bed back into place, and crept to the other side of the bedroom.

Neumann was still playing dumb and trying to appear accommodating. He asked the girl's name, what she looked like, and why they thought she was on board his boat. Someone mentioned a tracker and Bear cursed himself. He hadn't even thought to check Maria to see if she had been tagged. With an operation this large, they wouldn't want to chance losing any of their merchandise. He should've known better.

He eased the door open and started up the stairs. Along the wall was an eight-foot long steel gaff. He grabbed it with one hand while keeping himself steady with the other. The waves weren't too bad now that they were sitting still, but any noise he made would turn the tables on both him and Neumann and there'd be little time to react.

He paused at the top of the stairs, listened for voices.

"Look, I don't know who you're trying to find. I don't know why your tracker led to my boat."

"We will search it whether you are dead or alive," said the other man. "It's entirely up to you."

Bear didn't bother waiting for Neumann to come up with a clever line to either save his ass or buy them more time. The wheelhouse was between them. Bear exited the stairwell without being seen and snuck up behind one of the men holding a gun on Neumann.

He struck the guy on top of the head with the blunt end of the gaff. The man crumpled to the ground, his gun skittering across the deck. The second armed man had just enough time to turn in Bear's direction to see the pointed end of the gaff coming for his neck. He yelled out, but it was cut off by a wet gurgle of blood.

The third man tried to scramble for the pistol lying on the deck several feet away, but Bear pulled the gaff out of the man's neck and inserted it into the other man's chest in one swift move. In a matter of thirty seconds, all three men were incapacitated. Two of them were definitely dead.

The sound of the other boat's engine drew both Bear's and Neumann's attention. They watched as the driver cranked the wheel around, trying his best to escape. Neumann snatched the pistol from the deck and fired four rounds. The driver slumped over the wheel as at least three shots landed center mass. The boat drifted away, fading into the darkness.

Neumann looked down at his hand as he lowered the sidearm. "Been a while since I've had to do that."

Bear read ten different meanings in the look on the guy's face. "You all right?"

Neumann took a deep breath and nodded. "Never was my favorite part of the job. A lot of the guys like the violence and the power and the firearms. I just liked helping people. You know?"

Bear forced a half-spirited laugh. "Always knew you were a softie."

"Piss off." Neumann looked toward the stairs. "How's the girl?"

"She'll be all right. We need to find this tracker."

Bear descended the stairs while Neumann checked on the survivor. Maria crawled her way out of the tiny compartment behind the bed. She looked pale and sweaty, but no more so than usual. Symptoms of withdrawal? Or a reaction to the situation? The answer was somewhere in the middle.

She smoothed her hair back, plucking lingering strands. "Everything okay?"

"They're gone. Don't need to worry anymore."

"I heard gunshots. They're dead?"

"Most of them." Bear rubbed a hand across his beard. "They said something about a tracker."

Maria's eyebrows furrowed for a second and then her eyes

went wide. She grabbed the hem of her dress and felt along the edge until she came to a stop somewhere along the back.

"Here," she said. "I felt this before, earlier when they had first drugged me. I was panicking and happened to feel it while I was sitting down. I completely forgot about it."

He took the switchblade he had confiscated back at the house out of his pocket and cut a chunk of her dress away.

"It's not pretty, but it'll get the job done." He held up the bit of fabric and squeezed the tracker between his fingers. "And I know just what to do with this."

Chapter Twenty-Three

Bear and Maria emerged from below deck. A steady, salty breeze pelted their faces. Bear closed his eyes, breathed it in. He could taste it in the back of his throat.

Neumann had secured the unconscious man and left him by the stairs. He pointed to the two corpses at the stern. Bear told Maria to stay put, then headed back. He tied the bit of her dress with the tracker in it to one of the dead men's wrists. Then he threw both overboard before returning to Maria.

Neumann returned, wiping his brow. "Think we should've put the one with the tracker in a life preserver? The current would take him even further out to sea. Might take them longer to find him and figure out what's going on."

"Doesn't matter," Bear said. "There's enough blood that something will get to one of them sooner or later. Those guys will be pulling that tracker out of a shark's stomach before they realize we played them."

"Poor shark," Maria said.

Bear shrugged. "Best we can do."

Neumann opened the door to the wheelhouse. "We've got to get to land. Those guys likely radioed their position as soon as they spotted us. Whoever they were working for will find their vessel sooner rather than later and know something went sideways."

"You got a good place to land?" Bear asked.

"Maybe." Neumann looked up at the stars and then stared off to the southwest. "We can't go right into the port at Manila, but I've got a few other options. I'm just gonna need to figure out which one is going to cause the least amount of trouble."

"Let me know if you need anything," Bear said. "I'm going downstairs to interview our new guest."

"And me?" Maria said.

"Resting."

She said nothing. But a quick roll of her eyes gave her disposition away. She was ready to get back in the thick of it.

"I know it's frustrating," Bear said, descending the stairs, "but it's the best thing you can do for yourself right now."

She didn't argue. The fresh air seemed to have perked her up for a moment but feeling the heavy waves had turned her green again. Bear made sure she had everything she needed before he wandered off to the boiler room, where Neumann had tied the remaining pursuer to a large pipe. He was just starting to wake up when Bear entered the room.

"Morning, sunshine." Bear rolled his sleeves up to his elbows. "You speak English?"

The man blinked up at him for a moment, as though he was trying to bring Bear into focus. He looked smaller than the other men, but he was lean and muscular. He looked fast. Bear wasn't sure if he was also from North Korea, but he figured he'd get to that bit of information when it became relevant.

Once the man finished shaking away the fog in his head and realized where he was, he struggled against his bonds. But it was no use. Neumann had made sure the guy wasn't going anywhere.

"Look, I'm really not in the mood to repeat myself today." Bear squatted down in front of the man. "I hate flying and I spent twenty-four hours on a plane. Then I get to Hong Kong and have to fight a house full of idiots only to discover there's this girl there who's been sold as a sex slave." He paused and let disdain play out on his face. "Then I get on a boat, which—if I'm being honest—I'm not a huge fan of either. I had to squeeze into a tiny compartment and then crawl back out of it again just to kill three of your friends."

The man held his focus to the right of Bear's face.

Bear grabbed his chin and forced him to look at him, leveling him with a stare that would make most men tremble. "I've only had three hours of sleep. I'm tired. I'm hungry. And I'm inclined to just skip the small talk and go straight to the violence."

The man jerked his chin free of Bear's grasp and gazed at him unblinkingly. "I'll kill you."

"Oh good. You do speak English. I was worried this was gonna be difficult."

The man said nothing.

Bear got up and paced in front of his prisoner, rapping his knuckles against the wall before turning. "Okay, here's what I need to know. Who are you? Who do you work for? And, most importantly, what do you want with the girl?"

Again, the man didn't respond.

Bear pinched the bridge of his nose. His tear duct spilled back into his throat. He swallowed the saltiness down. "Look, man. I know you were just doing your job and all that. I know you can't tell me anything because then your boss will kill you." Bear squatted down in front of him again. "But the alternative here is that *I'll* kill you. If you tell me everything you know, I'll set you back on land and you'll have a chance to make a run for it."

The chugging of the engine and the clanging of the pipes

drowned out the man's ragged breaths. He dropped his chin to his chest and looked away.

Bear's patience ran out. He cocked his arm back and backhanded the guy across the cheek. There was a grunt and echo, but no other sound other than the ambiance of the room. So Bear aimed another blow at the man's face, though this time he hit a few inches to the left. And with his fist. The savage crunch of his nose was satisfying.

And still the man said nothing.

Every time Bear landed a blow, the man grunted a little bit, but he kept his teeth clenched against the pain. He wasn't going to say anything while Bear was employing kid shit. This was the minor leagues for a hired gun like him.

So Bear took the switchblade back out of his pocket and plunged it into the man's thigh without warning. Without negotiation. The scream that erupted from his throat was raw and primal. Despite his best effort to keep the pain off his face, the man's eyes welled up with tears.

"I told you I don't have time to play games." Bear pulled the knife from the man's leg and listened as he let out another scream. "And this is a lot less work than punching you in the face."

"Screw you," the man said, though this time his voice wavered with pain.

Bear aimed two inches above the previous wound and drove the knife into his leg one more time. Another scream. More tears. He was breathing hard in and out of his nose, trying to keep it together. He wasn't doing a very good job.

"What's your name?" Bear pulled the knife out and drew his arm back, aiming another two inches above the second wound. "I'm not going to ask again."

The man took two short, ragged breaths before he answered. "Kwang."

Bear held both hands out to the side. "Kwang, was that so hard?"

Kwang had a deadly look in his eye. He kept his mouth shut.

"Who do you work for? What do you want with the girl?"

"I can't tell you that."

Kwang's English was damn near perfect. His accent neutral. Why had they let the other man act as negotiator? Had Bear been too quick to kill the other man if he had been their leader?

Bear raised the knife again. "Don't make me ask a second time."

"I can't tell you—"

Bear didn't let him finish. He plunged the knife into the man's leg again, slowly making his way up his thigh, careful to avoid the femoral artery. A few more inches and he'd have to start working on the other leg.

"General Pyeong!" Kwang cried. "General Pyeong sent us to find her."

Bear left the knife in his leg for the time being. "Why?"

"He heard about a plot to kill him. Thought she might be involved."

Bear's knees were starting to hurt, but he stayed squatting in front of Kwang. "Why'd they think she's involved?"

"I don't know. Something about how they picked her up, I guess. It was too easy. Too perfect. They were being cautious."

"So they put a tracker on her."

Kwang nodded. The pain left him sweating and shaking. The knife wounds ran deep. His pants stained red with blood.

"Who did you expect to find on this boat?"

"Not a couple of Americans. We thought it'd be an inside job."

"The North Korean government?" Bear stared up at the ceiling. "Is he that paranoid?"

Kwang laughed. A desperate, humorless attempt. "Do you know anything about Nam-sun Choi?"

Newsreels spun through Bear's internal theater until he saw the headlines again. "He's the brother of Han Li Choi, current leader of North Korea. Died under mysterious circumstances not that long ago."

"There was nothing mysterious about it." Kwang looked down at his decimated leg and winced. "He was murdered. He was the eldest, the rightful leader of the country. General Pyeong only needed a single order to make the move."

"How many know General Pyeong was involved?"

"Only a few." Kwang wet his lips. "But apparently more than we thought."

Bear tried to process the information. This was much bigger than some sex trafficking ring. If General Pyeong thought Maria had been sent there to kill him, he wouldn't rest until he knew who was behind it, even if he hadn't been Maria's target.

It gave Bear some glimmer of hope, however. If the General was still after Maria, believing her to be the one sent to kill him, then he had no idea Sadie was the real threat. Presumably, that bit of misinformation was the only thing keeping her safe.

Kwang looked up at Bear. "If you sent her in, you should know about all of this already."

"I wasn't the one who sent her in," Bear said. "I was the one sent to retrieve her."

"Then who sent you?"

Bear didn't say it out loud, but he was thinking it.

Thorne.

If Thorne had sent Maria, then he also sent Sadie. And if he sent her, then he knew how Han Li's brother died. He was involved. No doubt in Bear's mind. And now the guy was desperately trying to clean up his own loose ends.

The thought sent a wave of pain through his gut. How much would Thorne try to pin on him?

Bear brought up a picture of Sadie on his phone. "Recognize her?"

Kwang waited a beat too long before answering. "Never seen her."

Bear ripped the knife out of his leg and waited until the scream faded. "I got no problem putting another three holes in you."

Kwang swallowed. "She looks a little familiar. Not many Americans in North Korea, you know?"

"Where is she now?"

"Same place," Kwang said. "In custody in North Korea."

Chapter Twenty-Four

Bear double-checked Kwang's bonds and headed back upstairs when he knew they would hold. Neumann waited for him in the wheelhouse. His cigar's cherry illuminated his face when he inhaled. Bear stepped into the smoky space inhaling the scent of chicory. He stared beyond the salt-stained window. A sliver of rose-gold light lined the horizon. Almost daylight.

Neumann looked down at Bear's knuckles. "Did you go easy on him?"

Bear wiped what little blood there was on his pants. "I decided to use alternative methods."

"I see." Neumann turned back to the wheel. "I don't miss it, you know."

"The job?"

"The violence." Neumann laughed. "You'd think I would've gotten used to it over the years. Instead I just got..."

"Tired?"

Neumann gave Bear a look like he was seeing him for the first time. "Yeah. You know the feeling?"

Bear shrugged. "Sometimes. Seen it in other guys, too."

Neumann bobbed his head up and down a few times and let the silence settle between them for a couple minutes before speaking again. "What the hell is going on, Riley?"

Bear sighed and rubbed the back of his neck. "I never should've dragged you into this. I'm sorry."

"Now, I didn't ask you to go and apologize. I knew when you called me up that it was going to be an interesting day. Didn't think it'd get this interesting, mind you, but I like a good surprise now and then. Keeps my heart young."

Bear chuckled. "Glad I could help."

"Seriously now. What did you get yourself mixed up in?"

"I wish I knew, Ernie. I wish I knew." Bear stared at the floor like he could see straight through the deck and into the room that held their prisoner. "This whole mess started in Costa Rica."

"You're a long way from Central America, son. How'd your sorry ass get dragged all the way over here?"

He looked over at Neumann. "It all started with Jack Noble."

Neumann threw his head back and laughed loud enough to make Bear forget his troubles. For just a moment, he was back at Ernie's house, sitting around the table with Jack and Neumann's wife. Ernie had made enough food to feed an army. Or at least two hungry privates and one woman with stage four cancer.

"I was gonna ask about Noble," Neumann said, wiping a tear from his eye. Bear wasn't sure if it was from the laughter or if Ernie had been reminiscing about that same night too. "But when he didn't show up with you, I figured maybe there was some bad blood there."

"Nah." Bear leaned back against the doorjamb and crossed his arms. "I mean, he's a pain in the ass and drags me into shit I'd rather avoid. But we're good. Just had to go our separate ways after

Costa Rica. I'll see him again soon enough. Maybe if I'm lucky he'll show up in North Korea."

Neumann's eyebrows disappeared into his hair. "North Korea?"

"Yeah, about that." Bear cleared his throat. "What kind of favor would I owe you if you dropped me off there?"

Neumann laughed, though this one had none of the good memories behind it. "No favor would cover that kind of trip. It's impossible."

Bear waved the comment away. "Nothing's impossible."

"We're a couple hours offshore from the Philippines. In another thirty minutes or so I'm going to call in a favor of my own so we don't have to dock in Manila." Neumann leaned forward and tapped one of the gauges in front of him. Bear saw the needle jump back to life. "But North Korea is a thousand miles away. And you can't exactly pull up along the coast expecting to be welcomed like an old friend."

"Was hoping you knew someone who could help us out."

He was pushing his luck. Neumann wouldn't hesitate to help him out of a jam, but cashing in all these favors was bad for business. His friend would be thinking about all the people he might not be able to save if he kept pulling on all these strings.

"Yeah, I know a guy." Neumann hadn't even hesitated. "We'll have to land in San Fernando first, but after that I think I can get someone to fly you to Korea."

"What'll the damage be?"

Neumann shrugged. "A couple bottles of vodka. The good stuff. It's an old friend. Someone who's itching for a little adventure these days. Shit, I bet he'll buy *me* the vodka."

"And you trust him?"

"With my life." Neumann made a minute adjustment to the steering wheel, then threw a glance over his shoulder. "In fact, I have trusted him with my life on more than one occasion. I'm still here, so that should tell you something."

Bear clapped Neumann on the shoulder. "Appreciate it. More than you'll ever know. And more than I'll ever be able to repay you."

"You take care of that girl, Riley." Neumann looked back out at the ocean. "She's tough. I know she can handle herself. And better than either of us could at that age. But that doesn't mean she should have to do it alone."

Bear nodded, a lump in his throat. He hadn't planned on keeping Maria around once they were back on land. He'd hoped Neumann would keep her close for a while. When he realized Neumann was no longer looking at him, he added, "Copy that."

Silence fell between them again. He wasn't sure if Neumann was thinking about his wife or the children they never had. Bear's thoughts had fallen on Sadie again.

This was turning into a wild goose chase, and Thorne was once again the pain in the ass at the center of it all.

He had half a mind to go downstairs and interrogate Maria a little more, but then he remembered everything she'd been through and his stance softened. Thorne may have created her, but that didn't mean she was anything like him.

Then again, Thorne had proven to be a master manipulator all along. Bear didn't trust him, and he'd be smart not to trust Maria either. Which meant he had to keep her close until this was all over. On the off chance something bigger was going on here, he had to be on guard.

Thorne got one over on him before.

It wouldn't happen a second time.

Chapter Twenty-Five

The sun hovered just above the horizon surrounding a white building atop a hill in fire when they pulled into San Fernando. The morning air was cool but soaked with dampness. The engines cut off and the sound of lapping waves filled the void.

A woman waited for them. She was severe in every sense of the word. Her black hair was pulled back into a tight bun. Her eyes were dark and hooded, and her lips were a harsh shade of red. Her pantsuit looked uncomfortably hot in the tropical climate, yet not a bead of sweat had formed on her smooth forehead.

She stood at the end of a dock, clipboard in hand.

Neumann seemed to gather himself before he called out to her, waving cheerfully and asking about her husband and kids. The woman answered in short, clipped tones before making Neumann sign something and stalking off in the opposite direction.

By the time Neumann made it back to the boat, Bear had already gotten it tied off and Maria had emerged from below deck.

"What's going on?" Her gaze followed the woman's retreating form. Even the way she walked looked rigid and uncomfortable.

"Ah, nothing." When Neumann caught both of them staring, he ran a hand through his hair. "Usually her husband meets me. Ramonda doesn't like me very much. Thinks what I do is distasteful."

"What'd you sign?" Bear asked.

"Just papers to show me coming and going. Officially, I'm just a fisherman who spends most of his days out on the sea. When I come back, I log my passengers as fish. No harm, no foul."

"As fish?" Maria raised an eyebrow. "And that works?"

Neumann shrugged. "Yeah. If we're ever caught, the consequences will be very expensive. Might even do some jail time. But Ramonda and her husband have a good reputation. The authorities trust they're being honest in their books."

Bear looked over Neumann's shoulder but couldn't spot the woman anywhere. "What exactly does she find distasteful?"

"She's a bit of a nationalist. Doesn't think I should be bringing the Chinese over here to the Philippines. She thinks I should just take them further inland and set them free like bunny rabbits."

"What a softie," Bear said.

"She has a little trouble getting the concept." Neumann clapped his hands together. "All right, grab your stuff and follow me. There's a car waiting. This favor comes with a little less attitude."

"What about our extra, uh, fish?" Bear asked.

It took a second for Neumann to register what Bear was saying. "Think you can keep him in line?"

Bear nodded.

"Then I'll have Charles pull up closer and we'll stuff him in the back. Not many cameras around here. I think we can avoid the major ones."

Bear didn't like taking chances, but he trusted Ernie to know what he was doing. If he said it was safe, then it was safe.

They traveled to Manila anyway to meet Neumann's friend with the plane. Was another Ramonda in the capital city, waiting for Neumann to arrive every week or two so she could glower at him? Or maybe the Manila Ramonda was the complete opposite: young, pleasant, and supportive of what Ernie was trying to do.

They had stuffed Kwang into the back of the SUV. Neumann pulled out a roll of duct tape and smoothed it over the man's mouth. The guy was still bleeding, but nothing significant enough to cause concern. If the driver was at all worried about the mess—or the fact that there was a man, bound and gagged, in the back of the car—he didn't mention it.

Neumann rode up front with their driver, Charles, and Maria and Bear took the back seat. It felt like he had just closed his eyes when she began shaking him awake. He sat up with a start.

"Relax." She leaned back, preparing to dodge an inadvertent blow. "We're here."

"Already?" Bear wiped the numbness from the side his face. "That was quick."

"It's been four hours." She seemed amused by his confusion. "Guess you needed it."

"Guess so."

He looked out the window expecting to see the sprawling city of Manila in front of him. Instead they were parked in front of a small cottage in the middle of nowhere. Bear turned to Neumann with a question already halfway out of his mouth.

"I thought we were—"

Neumann held up his hand. He looked agitated. "I'll explain when we get inside." He turned back to the driver and slipped him a wad of cash. "Get yourself some lunch. We'll be okay for a couple hours. I'll call when I need you again."

Charlie tipped his hat but remained silent. Neumann, Bear, and Maria slipped out of the car, and the two men pulled Kwang from the back. Together, they dragged him across the driveway and up the stairs with Maria trailing behind.

Bear looked over at his friend. "What is this place?"

Neumann kept looking straight ahead. "Falcon's house."

"Who's Falcon?"

"You're about to find out."

The four of them landed on the porch together, and before Neumann could knock on the door, it flung open and an old man appeared in the frame. He was half Bear's height and at best half his weight. His hair was shock white and he had a thin mustache framing his upper lip.

"Jesus, Mary, and Joseph," the man said. "Look at you, Ernest Neumann. You haven't changed a bit."

The man's eyes crinkled with his smile.

Neumann shifted Kwang's weight before answering. "Archibald, this is Riley Logan, the one I was telling you about."

"Call me Bear."

"Falcon," Archibald said. "Though I don't get to fly nearly enough these days."

"Yeah, I don't maul as many hikers as I used to either."

Falcon cracked a laugh and stood on his tiptoes to thump Bear on the shoulder. He looked over at Neumann. "I like him."

"Thought you might." Neumann nodded his head toward Maria. "And this is the girl. We're trying to get her somewhere safe."

"Well then, where are my manners? Come in." Falcon shuffled back through the door and led the way into his cabin. Neumann and Bear had to turn sideways so they could fit through the door with Kwang. Maria once again brought up the rear.

Falcon opened a door that led down to the cellar. "You can keep our guest down here. It's dry enough but not too comfortable. I assume he doesn't deserve the four-star treatment."

Bear looked over at Kwang. "Not really, no."

Kwang didn't put up too much of a struggle as they hauled him downstairs. He'd paled more. The blood loss was finally taking its toll. The more the guy struggled, the more he lost. He wasn't in any immediate danger, but at some point Bear would have to figure out what to do with him long-term.

By the time Neumann and Bear made it back up the stairs, Falcon had already brewed some tea and laid out cups for everyone. He pulled muffins out of the oven that spilled over the tins.

Bear walked over to Maria, who was sitting on the edge of the couch, cradling the cup of tea in her hands and blowing on it gently. "How're you holding up?"

She shrugged but didn't look up at him. Her gaze was distant. "All right, I guess."

"Your stomach okay?"

"A little wobbly, but better. Comes and goes. I've stopped sweating at least."

"Small miracles."

Falcon set a tray of muffins on the coffee table in front of them. "There's a shower in the back. You're welcome to use it."

Maria gave him a sad smile and set her teacup down. "Thanks. I could use it."

Neumann handed her a bundle of clothes he'd pulled from the boat prior to their departure. She retreated to the bathroom with a quiet thanks.

"I'm worried about her," Neumann said, picking up a muffin and pretending to inspect it.

"She'll be all right," Bear said. "She's strong, remember?"

"Everyone has their breaking point."

Falcon took a loud sip from his own teacup. "Too true, too true."

There was a beat of silence. Bear didn't usually find breaks in conversation awkward, but there was clearly something hanging between Neumann and Falcon. He stared at Ernie waiting for the next move.

Neumann put the muffin back on the tray and leveled a look at Falcon. "I don't want you flying them to North Korea."

Falcon's smile didn't fade despite Neumann's sentiments. "Then you shouldn't have called me."

"I called you to see if you knew anyone who could get them in without being detected."

"I do know someone."

"Other than yourself."

Falcon's eyes twinkled. "I'm the best pilot on this island. The best one in all of Asia."

Bear couldn't tell if it was true or just an old man's bluster. He turned to Neumann. "Why don't you want him to fly?"

It was Bear's turn to get leveled with a stare now. "No offense to my good friend here, but he's getting a little up there in years."

"I'm as healthy now as I was at twenty-two." Falcon's voice rose and his tone was sharp.

"I don't doubt that, Archie, but who knows what the hell could happen."

"That's what makes it so fun." Falcon raised his hands when he saw the deadly look Neumann gave him. "In all honestly, I only know a couple of pilots who would dare to get you close to North Korea, and none of them are here. It might take them weeks to put their affairs in order."

Sadie flashed in Bear's mind. He gripped his cup tight, ignoring the heat. "We don't have weeks. We don't even have days."

Falcon took another loud sip from his tea and sat up a little straighter. "I'm prepared to leave in a couple hours."

Neumann pinched the bridge of his nose. "Archie."

Falcon set his cup down on the table hard enough for some of the tea to slosh over the side. His eyes flashed. "Now you listen here, boy. I've been flying longer than you've been alive. You need a favor and I'm willing to give you one. It's the right thing to do. A little danger never stopped me before."

Bear liked Falcon's gumption but needed to make sure the old man knew what he was getting himself into. "I've got a lot of people on my tail. You don't need to pay for my sins."

The twinkle in Falcon's eye returned. "If you want, you can owe me a favor, too. But I gotta warn you. I'm older than I look. I won't have too much time to cash in on it."

That didn't make Bear feel better.

Falcon drained the remainder of his tea and stood up. "You need a pilot. A good one. Luckily for you, I'm a great one. I'll get you closer to the North Korean border than anyone else willing to make the trip. And we'll do it with a bottle of vodka in our hands."

Neumann turned to Bear. "I told you he'd be the one giving *us* the vodka."

Bear chuckled and stood up. His hand swallowed Falcon's whole as they shook on the deal. "Sounds like a good time to me."

Chapter Twenty-Six

The plan was simple. Maria was still too sick to be in the field, so she volunteered to stay behind. Neumann had no interest in leaving the Philippines and risking his life in Korea. He had refugees to think about. But he did tell Bear he'd watch over Maria and try to get some additional information out of Kwang.

Keep her close.

He'd prefer to watch over her himself, but Neumann would suffice.

Energy spilled out of Falcon from the moment he stepped into his plane to the minute they landed in China. The small aircraft caused Bear to feel every pocket of air, and every time the plane rose, fell, or pitched to the side. He clenched and unclenched his fists, tightened and released muscle groups, and slowed his breathing down, which was painful at times. By the time they were on the ground, he was willing to walk into North Korea with no weapons and no plan if it meant he'd never have to fly again.

Falcon had access to a private airfield in Dandong, adjacent to the northwest corner of North Korea. When Bear deplaned, there was a Jeep Wrangler waiting for him with the keys in the ignition. He turned to Falcon and stuck out his hand.

"It was a pleasure to meet you."

"Likewise." Falcon's smile was framed by his thin mustache and his eyes crinkled at the corners. "I might've given him grief back there, but Ernest was right. I'd love to get out there and go with you, but I'm just getting too old."

"Maybe, maybe not." Bear opened the door to the Wrangler. "You're still one hell of a pilot."

"I appreciate that." Falcon's eyes drooped just a little bit. "You gonna be okay, son? You got a plan?"

"Half a one anyway." He threw the bag of supplies that Falcon had given him into the passenger seat and slid behind the wheel. "The smartest play will be to cross the Yalu River before the sun comes up. Should be frozen enough to drive right across."

"Should be?" Falcon's lips twitched with concern.

Bear looked out over the dashboard like he could see the river from miles away. "Frozen enough. They won't be expecting anyone to make that trip."

"And for good reason. Isn't there another way?"

"There are plenty of other ways" Bear shut the door between them and rolled down the window. "But this is the only one that gives me a decent chance of making it across without being caught."

Falcon took a deep breath and blew it out slowly. His visible breath rose like smoke and disappeared into the air above his head. Then he reached into the car to shake Bear's hand. "In that case, good luck and Godspeed. You're gonna need all the help you can get."

Bear put the Wrangler in first gear and looked back at Falcon before taking off. "Don't I know it."

G etting to the river wasn't an issue. Bear turned his lights off before it was in sight. No point in making it that easy for them. The full moon lit up his path. After a few short minutes his eyes adjusted to the darkness. He kept the pace slow and steady. It'd be stupid to make a mistake this close to the border.

The river appeared and his pulse quickened twenty beats per minute at least. He'd picked an area away from border towns and bridges. He didn't want to risk running into a checkpoint or being spotted by local villagers who might be getting paid to keep their eyes out for anyone trying to escape North Korea.

The Yalu River wasn't particularly wide in most places, but Bear had to sacrifice the notion of a quick hop, skip, and a jump through the water in order to be in a more secluded location. Where he was sitting now was less than a quarter of a mile wide, but if he couldn't make it across in the Jeep, he'd be SOL on the other side.

And half-frozen.

Bear sat in the darkness a half-hour before making his move. In that time he let his eyes further adjust to the landscape. There was no movement, animal or human, and he didn't spot any lights in the distance. As far as he could tell, he was in complete solitude.

The frozen river glistened in the moonlight, looking like a silver blanket stretching out in front of him. It was bitterly cold, but he also knew that the thickness of the ice would depend on the depth of the river. If he had made a mistake and picked an area that wasn't shallow enough, that meant the ice would break away and he'd be soaked to the bone. It wouldn't kill him—right away at least. But if he lost the car, chances were that he'd barely make it to the other side before hypothermia set in.

He performed one last scan of his surroundings and then flicked on the Jeep's fog lights. The sudden brightness made him squint, but he pushed through the pain and waited another couple minutes before he was used to it. It was a risk to have the lights on at all, but he'd rather see what lay ahead of him than all of a sudden find himself under the ice without so much as a warning.

When he was sure he was alone, Bear hopped out of the Wrangler and walked over to the edge of the bank. He tested the shallows with his full body weight. It'd be uncomfortable if he broke through, but the worst that would happen is he'd wind up with wet socks.

The ice held.

He slid one foot forward, and then the next, until he was several feet from the shore. His weight was nothing compared to the Wrangler's, but the ice didn't so much as pop in protest against his invasion. Maybe this would end up being the easiest part of the journey so far.

Bear muttered under his breath. "Don't get ahead of yourself just yet."

After standing out there for a few minutes Bear made his way back to the Jeep and hopped in. He coaxed the Wrangler into four-wheel-drive and left it in first gear, then took his foot off the gas. A Wrangler will roll on when configured as such, straight ahead or up a cliff, so long as it doesn't tip backward…

…or fall through the ice.

The Jeep rolled forward, the hum of the engine sounding more and more like the quiet purr of a content kitten.

The knobby tires crunched across the thin layer of snow that had settled over the ice. He held his breath until all four tires were off solid ground and were inching their way across the frozen river.

The fog lights made it difficult to look directly at the ice in front of him. He stared on and waited for his eyes to adjust. If there was even a single crack, he could go under in a matter of seconds. He'd have to decide whether or not to throw the Jeep in reverse or floor it, hoping he could get to the other side before the river's icy claws dragged him under.

Bear tugged his coat around him a little tighter and sat up straight behind the wheel. The lights washed out the surrounding darkness. With it so bright right in front of him, he wouldn't have a chance in hell of spotting someone or something crawling out of the shadows.

He was operating on pure, dumb luck.

Luckily most people were trying to escape North Korea, not break into it. Another problem was that once he got into the country, he would stick out like a sore thumb. Even worse than in Hong Kong. At least China was used to Americans coming and going for business deals. North Koreans were bound to start whispering.

And in a land of silence, whispers were deafening.

Bear hoped he could get to where he needed to go before he was spotted and detained. He tried not to think about the fact that he didn't have an escape route. Falcon had offered to stick around and pick him back up in Dandong, but Bear had turned him down. There was no point in both of them getting caught if things went sideways.

The plan was straightforward. Get in, find Sadie, and get back across the border. If he could manage that, he was fairly certain he'd be able to find a way back to the Philippines. Of course, that was easier said than done.

A crackle and a pop startled Bear out of his thoughts about eventually making it back home to the States. He looked over at the satellite phone that Neumann had provided. The plan was to call them back at Falcon's cottage, which was their temporary home base, once Bear was safe. Neumann was working on getting more information from Kwang. Information that Bear would need in order to find Sadie.

But Bear had purposefully kept the sat phone off in case he was trying to hide out. The last thing he needed was for it to go off and give away his location.

So when Bear heard another strange pop, he knew it was the ice beneath his wheels.

He took a deep breath, and then popped his driver's side door open wide enough to look down at the ice. The ice illuminated in the moonlight. There were several thin cracks crawling out like a spiderweb from beneath his wheels.

The river was deeper out here away from the shore, which meant it was harder to freeze even in the dead of winter. He had tried to take that into consideration, calculating the best area to cross by making sure it wasn't wider or too deep and still far enough from civilization.

Bear gently closed his door, afraid that even the sound of it clicking shut would be enough to send him plummeting through the frozen terrain. He looked out over his hood and watched the ice bathed in light. He hadn't spotted it at first, as blinding as the light was, but sure enough, there the cracks were.

He didn't allow himself to panic. He squinted at the far side of the river, trying to gauge how far he'd gotten before the ice had started to crack. He wasn't even halfway yet, which meant he wasn't to the deepest part of the river where the thinnest ice would be.

His knuckles turned white as he gripped the wheel. He kept his foot on the floor next to the accelerator to prevent himself from speeding up or panicking and hitting the brake. If he slowed the Jeep down, chances were the ice would give way almost immediately. His momentum was the only thing keeping him dry. But if he sped up, there was a chance the tires might slip on the ice. Once they caught again, it might be enough to shatter it completely.

Rolling his head from one side to the other, he cracked the vertebrae in his neck until he felt looser and calmer. But it didn't drown out the popping of the ice outside the car. He pushed against his door and peered down at the ice beneath his tires.

It looked slick with water. Which only meant one thing—the ice was giving way.

Bear toed the gas pedal just a little bit, sending the Wrangler forward an extra three miles an hour. Peering through the windshield, he figured he'd crossed the halfway point about a minute or two ago. A quarter of a mile was starting to feel like the longest marathon of his life.

He kept his door propped open, hoping it would provide him enough warning should something start to give. It wouldn't be much, but he preferred the idea of launching himself out of the Jeep and onto the ice a couple feet away instead of going down with the Wrangler.

The Jeep rocked to the right. Bear looked down in time to see the tip of a rock sticking out of the water like the tip of an iceberg. When the water was flowing, it created quite the eddy in the middle of the river. But with the water frozen, it had been impossible to spot.

The Wrangler could handle driving over a little rock, but the ice wasn't as sturdy. As soon as the Jeep's tire connected with the ground again, the ice split beneath the wheel and he was jostled to the side. If he had been on solid ground, he wouldn't have even noticed the movement. It was par for the course when you were driving over roots and stones or even potholes on an asphalt road.

But Bear was hyper attuned to everything going on around him. When the ice gave the final pop and he saw the water bubble up to the surface, Bear pushed his foot down a little harder on the gas and prayed that the tires wouldn't lose traction.

The noise as the ice shifted was deafening in the night air. Had anyone else heard it? Doubtful. Not out here. And even if they did, he didn't care. He could fight off anyone who came looking for him. It was improbable that he could fight off hypothermia.

So when his driver's side wheel started going under, Bear shifted into second and slammed the accelerator down the rest of the way and listened as the engine revved in response. He slammed his door shut, gripped the wheel until his hands hurt, and made a beeline for the shore.

Chapter Twenty-Seven

Though the trip lasted a few minutes at most, it felt like hours. Bear counted down every foot he got closer to the bank, and just as he felt the back end of the Wrangler dip down past the ice and into the water, the front end hit land and nearly launched him out of his seat. His head slammed against the roof. His elbow smacked the door hard enough he thought it might've broken. None of that mattered. The pain faded. He was on dry ground.

Bear cut the lights and engine. As it cooled off, it ticked louder and louder. He waited until his eyes adjusted to the darkness before he hopped out. The cold penetrated his clothing, freezing his sweat-soaked skin.

He did a once over of the Jeep and everything seemed to be in order. The water on the backend of the car was already starting to frost over, reminding Bear just how lucky he was.

A branch snapped off to his left. He spun in that direction and reached for a gun that wasn't there. He had left his weapons in the vehicle.

His heart pounded against his ribcage. He stood as still as possible. If he was lucky, whoever was out there didn't have night vision. Without that he'd be hard to spot even with the moon shining as brightly as it was. Leave him enough of a chance to duck and run. Or if he was less lucky, take a bullet and live to tell about it.

After several minutes in the frigid night air with his hands going numb and his muscles locking up, nothing happened. At that point Bear decided getting shot might be better than freezing to death, so he took one step backward, then two, and headed for the Jeep. No shots rang out. Must've been nothing more than an animal scurrying through the undergrowth.

He climbed inside and cranked the heat up and dug out the satellite phone. After powering it on he called Neumann, hoping his night was going a little better. Static on the line nearly drowned out the ringing. The other end clicked. Silence.

"It's me. I made it."

There was an audible sigh of relief from the other end. It was Neumann. "Good. How's Falcon?"

"He was good when I left him." Bear opened and closed his left hand, trying to get the blood pumping again. "He promised not to wait around for me."

"I'm surprised he didn't convince you to let him tag along."

Bear chuckled. "He tried. But he knew I needed him in the plane more than I needed him on the ground."

"Crazy-ass old bastard," Neumann said. "He's worse than a two-year-old."

"How's Maria?"

"She's good." Neumann's voice faded. "She's lying down again. I think the symptoms have almost passed, but she's still exhausted."

"What about our other friend?"

Neumann's voice hardened. "Oh, he's doing great. Been singing all morning."

"You haven't lost your touch, I see."

"Sometimes I wish I had," Neumann said. "But not today. You ready?"

"Hit me."

Neumann drew in a deep breath. "You're lucky you picked where you did to cross. These guys were staying at a house just over the border. About three or four miles to the south. He says there's a couple men stationed there, heavily armed."

"Anything more about our missing friend?"

"No." There was some rustling in the background. "I don't think this guy had a high enough pay grade. Just a dumb grunt. Didn't trust him with a lot of information."

"And you believe him?" Bear switched the phone into his other hand and started opening and closing his right, trying to get some feeling back into that one now. "Could be lying."

"I'll pretend you meant no disrespect by doubting my bullshit meter."

"Hey, it's my life on the line here."

"I know, I know." Neumann's voice was serious now. "How was crossing the river?"

"Let's just say I plan on finding an alternative route out." He stared out the driver's side window, scanning the terrain. He didn't see any movement. "All right hit me with the coordinates for the house. It's time to end this."

Bear kept his lights down and his foot off the gas as he slowly wound his way across the North Korean countryside. Brake lights would be as bright as headlights at night, and as loud as the engine already was, he wasn't trying to make it worse. The trip dragged on, but it was the best way to stay under the radar.

The house was smaller than the one in Hong Kong. A single

story painted off-yellow, and one visible entrance. Kwang had told Neumann there could be up to four people inside, but Bear wasn't going to take any chances.

The house sat on the corner of a quiet street. This was rural North Korea, which meant neighbors were far enough away that if there was a shootout, they might not hear it. Or at the very least, it would give Bear a chance to hightail it out of there if the authorities were called in.

But the longer he sat watching the house, the more he was convinced it was empty. The lights were off, there were no cars in the driveway, and not a single person could be seen anywhere in the vicinity.

The question now was whether or not Kwang had given them bad intel.

Bear decided to call Neumann back after he checked out the house. He opened the door to the Wrangler and stepped out onto the road. Silence. In the summer the air would be filled with the sounds of nature's nightlife. But now it was just filled with the absence of sound.

With no streetlamps, it was easy for Bear to keep to the shadows. When he reached the front door, he stopped and listened. Still nothing. That's when he noticed the door was already cracked a couple inches.

As he pushed the door open wide, he knew he wouldn't find a soul in there. The house had been scrubbed clean. There were no pictures or knick-knacks on the walls. No tables or chairs or furniture of any kind. There were only a handful of rooms, and each one was empty like it was move-in day.

Bear pulled out the sat phone and dialed Neumann.

"The house is clear."

"How many were there?"

"Nah, I mean it's clear. There's nothing here. Literally nothing. Not even dust on the floor."

There was momentary static while Neumann answered, making him sound robotic. "You think the intel was bad?"

"Smells like stale smoke. Someone was definitely here. But they had plenty of time to clear out. I'm not going to find any leads."

"Must've gotten spooked when their guys didn't come back from their little fishing trip. Especially if they managed to find that tracking device."

Bear rubbed the back of his neck. "Now what?"

"Let's ask our friend."

Bear could hear Neumann open the door to the basement and descend the creaky stairs. There was a grunt and a muffled grumble before Bear heard Neumann loud and clear.

"All right, get up. The house was a bust."

"What do you mean it was a bust?" Kwang sounded tired. Bear couldn't tell if it was from lack of sleep or lack of blood.

"It was empty." Neumann paused and dropped his voice until it sounded low and dangerous. "Did you lie to us?"

"No, no. They must've left when we didn't come back." Kwang grunted like he was trying to shift into a more comfortable position. "I thought they would still be there."

"Where would they go if you guys didn't return?"

"I don't know. Could be anywhere."

Neumann sighed. He sounded almost as tired as Kwang. "Look, son, I finally got your blood out of my favorite shirt. I don't want to do laundry again tonight, so *tell me what the backup plan was.*"

Kwang groaned. "There's another house in the next town over. I can give you the coordinates."

There was a smile in Neumann's voice. "You ready, Bear?"

Bear couldn't help the smile on his face either. "I'm ready."

Chapter Twenty-Eight

Bear sat outside the safe house the next town over. He could've found the place without the coordinates. It was small, like the first one, but where the one from before had been completely deserted, this one was occupied.

There were two cars out front, nothing flashy or suspicious. He parked the Wrangler down the road and hopped out, his 9mm in hand. Again, there were no streetlights, but he avoided being out in the open for too long. Some passing clouds dimmed the moon for a few minutes, but if someone was looking for movement, they'd be able to spot it.

The house was lit up. He couldn't tell how many people were inside, but going off the cars alone, there could be at least eight. He'd had worse odds in a fight before, and he held the element of surprise, but he wasn't looking to take any unnecessary risks. It's not like he had any contacts he could hit up if he got into trouble.

The front door opened and two men exited the house. One of them immediately lit a cigarette, took a deep breath, and blew the smoke straight up into the air. He had a pistol in his other hand, aimed at the ground.

The second man took his job much more seriously. He stepped outside the light emanating from the windows at the front of the house and peered intently into the darkness. Bear shifted his body closer to the tree he was hiding behind. It was large enough to keep even his large frame from view, but he was feeling more paranoid than usual.

The second man had some sharp words for the first, who rolled his eyes and took another drag from his cigarette. The cherry lit up bright. He kept it hanging loose from his mouth and he checked his weapon and followed his partner into the night. They started to do a perimeter sweep in the opposite direction from Bear's position.

Perfect.

He waited until they turned the corner to creep out from his hiding spot. He paused long enough to make sure no one was watching from the house, then dashed across the front yard, stopping short of turning the same corner.

He could hear their muffled footsteps in the grass. One of them had a slow and steady gait. That was the second guy. The first guy would walk forward, stop, and blow cigarette smoke from his mouth. Then do it all over again.

Bear risked peeking around the corner. Sure enough, the man with the cigarette was only a few feet away while the other one was close to the other end of the house. He didn't wait for his partner to join him before he turned the corner, so Bear made his move.

He waited until the man with the cigarette flicked it away before reaching around and covering his mouth with one hand. With the other, Bear knocked the man's pistol away. It landed with a soft thud on the ground. He wrapped his arm around the man's neck, squeezed, pulled, and twisted it sharply to the right. Then he let the body thud to the ground.

He picked up the man's pistol as he crept forward. There were several windows lining this side of the house, two of which weren't covered by curtains. He didn't risk taking a look inside just yet. He still needed to get rid of the other patrol.

Just as Bear was turning the corner at the other end of the house, the remaining patrolman said something in Korean and casually looked over his shoulder. It took him a second to register that Bear was standing there instead of his partner. He had just enough time to shout something in Korean before Bear threw a right hook that caved in the side of the guy's face. The man crumpled to the ground in a heap of limbs.

Shouts from inside told Bear he'd been compromised. He shot the man on the ground twice in the head to make sure he wouldn't pop up and attack him from behind. If he didn't already have the attention of everyone inside, he surely did now.

Someone threw open the back door to check what was going on outside. Their mistake. Bear wasted no time putting one bullet in his chest and another right in the center of his forehead. He fell to the ground, wedging the back door open with his body.

Bear had a line of sight on another man inside the house, but he was also staring down the barrel of a rifle. He dove to the side before bullets started flying his direction, tearing through the paneling on the house.

There were more shouts from inside, and then the scraping of furniture as someone made their way over to the door. Bear figured they thought they'd hit him, so he stood up and extended his arm until his gun was just the right height to be held to someone's head. As soon as the man emerged, gun drawn, Bear pulled the trigger and down the guy went on top of his associate.

The man inside with the rifle opened fire again. A bullet a second. Bear didn't wait for it to stop. He sprinted around the far side of the house and peered in through one of the windows. The only movement he saw was from the man with the rifle. Bear lined up his shot and pulled the trigger. The sound of gunfire choked off, but it left a distinct ringing in his ears.

He did a body check, starting with his head and moving down his torso, then his arms, and finally his legs. He was a little banged up, but there were no bullet wounds. No pain so intense that he thought he might have twisted or fractured something. He was in one piece.

He kept circling the house until he was back out front. Pistol at the ready, he kicked down the door and cleared the room just in case someone had been hiding in the corner. The first time he walked through the tiny house he made sure both the bedroom and the bathroom were clear. The second pass he was looking for clues.

Somehow all of this was tied up with Thorne. It was Thorne who had recruited him to find Sadie. Instead, he found Maria, who had been working with Thorne to take down a sex trafficking ring. Sadie had been kidnapped by the same people, and it sounded like Thorne was trying to tie up loose ends by taking out General Pyeong.

But why was Sadie involved? She wouldn't have volunteered to work with Thorne again. Perhaps Thorne had control over Sadie's superiors and had convinced them to send her. But why was Thorne so hell-bent on taking out some random North Korean General?

Bear shook his head. He felt like he was getting nowhere. It didn't help that he kept shuffling around the same room, too distracted by his thoughts to see anything in front of him.

If Thorne was trying to get rid of Pyeong to cover his tracks in the assassination of the current North Korean dictator's brother, there were really only two reasons why. One, he was exacting revenge for a betrayal, or two, he was covering up any involvement the U.S. may have had in the operation.

But was Thorne really in charge, or was someone pulling *his* strings and forcing him to clean up a mess he created? Bear loved the idea that someone had power over Thorne—just as long as that person didn't set their sights on him. His life was interesting enough as it was.

He walked over to the back door and dragged the dead bodies inside. Someone would be by soon enough once these guys didn't check in, but he didn't want to give even the distant neighbors reason to be suspicious.

As he started to close the door, he heard what sounded like muffled shouting. It sounded close enough that he drew his weapon and shielded himself behind the door. As the shouting continued it sounded less like it was coming from across the yard and more like it was coming from…beneath him.

Bear kept his pistol drawn as he stepped outside and followed the shouts to a small wooden door set into the ground at the base of the house. It was dirty enough that he hadn't noticed it when he was out there earlier.

That, and he was getting shot at.

Cellars like these were often no more than a deep, narrow hole in the ground used to keep vegetables and canned goods cool and fresh. But the yelling coming from inside indicated that there were more than just potatoes down there.

He aimed his pistol at the door with one hand and yanked the thick chain holding the doors together. The lock was open. He discarded it, freed the chain, and opened the hatch. It was dark, but the moon still shone bright enough to reveal a figure bound and gagged in the middle of the dank room.

As soon as the yelling had started, Bear kept a thought—that he'd find the one person he had been looking for this entire time —at bay.

But as soon as the woman looked up at him, he knew that luck had been on his side. Despite the darkness of the night and the dirt smeared across her face, Bear had no trouble deciphering who it was.

A wave of relief flooded his body as he said her name.

"Sadie."

Chapter Twenty-Nine

Bear stumbled down the final couple stairs in his rush to reach Sadie. He caught himself and pulled the gag from her mouth and immediately got to work on the knots in the rope that bound her hands behind her. Then the ones around her ankles.

The mold in the cellar assaulted his lungs. It was all he could smell. Every part of his respiratory system burned. He slowed his breathing down to avoid taking too much in.

"Bear." Her voice was raw and quiet, like she had been screaming for some time. Or perhaps the mold had done its number on her. Her eyes were wide, mouth hung open. Half shock, half relief. Tears wet her eyes.

"One more knot," he said, pulling the last of the rope from her legs. He wrapped an arm around her waist and gently maneuvered one of her arms over his shoulder. "Can you walk?"

"Yeah." She stood up with his help and winced. She hobbled forward. "I don't think anything's broken. Just banged up a bit."

Bear had trouble keeping his emotions in check. He and Sadie weren't old friends by any means, but after everything they'd gone through together in Costa Rica, he felt like he'd already known her a lifetime. He had never allowed himself to ponder the possibility, but until that moment, he never realized how much he had been preparing to find her dead body.

They had to turn sideways to get up the narrow staircase. Sadie's legs gave way as soon as they hit the lawn. Bear scooped her up into his arms and took her inside the house. He laid her down on the couch and made her drink two glasses of water before he let her talk.

Sadie placed the empty glass on the table and turned toward him, staring like she didn't believe he was really there.

"Can't thank you enough, Bear."

"Sure you're not hurt?"

She ran a hand down each arm, then each leg, then rubbed the back of her neck. "Pretty sure. Couple of bruises, couple of shallow scrapes, nothing major. Hard to breathe, but ribs feel intact."

"Ton of mold down there. Bet it did a number on your lungs."

"That, and they tried to beat information out of me. Felt like they were going easy though. Don't think they knew how much I could handle."

"Thank God for that." Bear got up to fill her glass again. He didn't know what she needed. A nurse? A friend? Nothing at all? He handed her the water but didn't sit back down. Any relief at finding her had been taken over by his drive to push forward again.

She took a sip and put it back on the table. "You're hovering."

"We need to get you out of here. I got someone that can pick us up over the border. He'll fly us to the Philippines. From there we can get back to the States."

Sadie stood up with a groan. "I appreciate that...but...no."

"No?"

Chapter Thirty

Bear spent the next twenty minutes filling Sadie in on everything, from his time on St. Lucia and Derek and Sophia's deaths, to his imprisonment and Thorne's visit.

He told her about Hong Kong and the flight over. About stumbling across Maria. About calling up Neumann and running into the Korean men at sea.

She soaked it all up like a solid field operative would.

"Right now, Neumann is back at Falcon's place with Maria and Kwang." He waved the satellite phone in the air between them. "I'm going to call him and see if we can't get a ride out of here sooner rather than later."

"No." She crossed her arms over her chest. "I'm not going anywhere until this is done."

Bear took a moment before responding. "My mission was to get you. I did that. We're not involved in this mess. We don't owe Thorne anything."

"But my mission isn't over," she said. "I didn't get to do what I came here to do."

"And you know Thorne was behind that. Do you really want to play right into his hands?"

She shrugged. "You don't know that the order came from him. And even if it did, don't you want to know what he's up to?"

"I already know what he's up to. He's waiting for me to do his dirty work. I'm not going to give him the satisfaction."

Sadie held her hands up in surrender. "I understand what you're saying, but how long were you and Jack looking for Thorne before he finally cornered you in New York?"

"I wouldn't say *cornered* us. But it was at least a couple months."

"And nothing from him until he showed up at the prison." She ran her fingers through her hair again. "My point is that he's always one step ahead of you. Now's your chance to be one step ahead of him. We don't have to do his dirty work for him, but let's at least find out what his dirty work entails."

Bear tipped his head back and looked up at the cigarette-smoke stained ceiling for a moment. "How did you even know about New York anyway?"

"Jack told me." Her gaze flitted away from his for a second and then came back. "He calls me every once in a while."

Bear didn't think it was right to pry. Instead, he asked, "You got a plan?"

"Not exactly." she looked back down at the phone they found in the house. "But if we can figure out where to find General Pyeong, maybe we can play the two sides against each other."

"Have Thorne and Pyeong incriminate themselves," he said.

She smiled. "Two birds with one stone."

A chime sounded from the burner phone. Both of them looked down at it. After a second's hesitation, Sadie opened the text and showed it to him. Just like the others, it was in Korean and he couldn't read a single word of it.

He was wondering how accurate an internet translation would be when they heard the crunch of gravel outside. He and Sadie froze and made eye contact for a split second before they both jumped up and pressed themselves against the front wall, each trying not to disturb the curtains too much as they moved them to the side to get a better view of their visitor.

"I spot two of them," she said.

"Same here." He waited until the second man exited the car. The guy lit a cigarette and looked back over his shoulder at the deserted street. "I don't think they know what happened here. Look at 'em. They're too relaxed."

"Two of us, two of them." Sadie was looking around presumably for a weapon. "We could take them. Especially if we have the element of surprise."

"That element is only going to last until they realize their guys aren't breathing anymore." Bear glanced over at Sadie to see if she'd chastise him for not cleaning up after himself. "You sure you'd be up for a fight anyway?"

"Their friends tied me up and beat me nearly every day for a week." She grabbed a decapitated table leg off the ground. She tested the heft, and then looked up at him with a glint in her eye. "I could use a fight."

He peeked behind the curtain again and noticed the guy smoking the cigarette turn to his left and peer into the darkness. He said something to his partner, then headed in that direction. The other guy raised his fist to knock on the door.

"Guess we're doing this," Bear said, and then whipped open the door.

The man on the other side froze. He had just enough time to drop his mouth open in surprise before Bear punched him in the throat. A stifled scream escaped no more audible than a cricket's fart. Bear kicked out the man's right knee and sent him to the ground.

Meanwhile, Sadie leapt over the guy on the stoop and took off after the man who'd been smoking the cigarette. Bear saw him reach for the gun on his hip, but he barely got it clear of his holster before Sadie knocked it from his hand with the table leg. She followed up with a kick to the groin and a knee to the face, and he went down just as quickly as his friend.

Bear should've been watching his own man, but Sadie was a sight to behold when she was kicking ass. He felt the guy at his feet shift and looked up just in time to see the glint of a knife. The man attempted to thrust it straight into Bear's thigh, but he managed to grab the guy's arm, twist it around, and plunge it into his neck. If that didn't do it, then the weight of Bear's knee into the man's chest would. Blood exploded from an artery and the man bled out in a matter of seconds.

The sound of struggling made Bear turn back to Sadie, who had pulled her guy's arm behind his back and pinned him to the ground with her knee.

She looked up at him with a little bit of a manic glint in her eye. "You were supposed to keep him alive."

Bear wiped his hands on the other man's shirt and then stood up. "We only need one of them."

Sadie's prisoner started to struggle, so she jacked his arm up even higher. He immediately stopped moving. "Does that mean we've got a plan?"

"Part of one anyway."

"Works for me."

Chapter Thirty-One

The plan was straightforward. Bear and Sadie tied up their prisoner, and after about ten minutes of threats and a couple of right hooks, forced him to divulge the information in the most recent text message.

It was an address of a nearby military facility. It didn't take long for Sadie and Bear to decide it was their next logical move. If the general wasn't there himself, they would at least be one step closer to finding someone who could summon him.

Bear and Sadie left the man tied to a chair inside the house, and then commandeered his car to make the drive over to the base.

Sadie stared out the window for a solid ten minutes before turning back to him. "I don't think this is the smart play."

"It's definitely not the smart play." Bear checked his rearview. The deserted street offered little comfort. It wasn't hard to remember that he was in rural North Korea, but he still expected to see headlights barreling toward him. "But I'm tired of waiting around for Thorne to get another leg up on us, and General Pyeong is our best chance at finally taking him down."

"They're gonna spot us a mile away." She looked down at the map she had open on her lap. "Take your next right."

He took the corner a little sharp and Sadie had to right herself. "They'll be expecting one of these cars. Might give us a few seconds to get the jump on them."

"A few seconds isn't that much time."

"It's all we've got." He felt reckless and tried to rein it in. He didn't mind putting his own life on the line, but he didn't want to do that to Sadie. Especially not after everything she'd been through the last couple of months. "Besides, if we can convince them we're not a threat, we might get a face-to-face with the general. And if that happens, we have a shot at getting him to work with us against Thorne."

"Those are a couple of big ifs. Christ, we're walking into the lion's den holding a slab of steak. What are the chances they don't look at us as a threat?" Sadie paused and traced her finger along their route on the map. "Take that left up there and then stay straight. We've got another ten miles before we get to the base. It looks like it's all pretty open except for a patch of trees to the west. We can try driving into that if it's not too dense."

He nodded his head but didn't say anything. He knew she was right. Best case scenario, they get into the base and find General Pyeong without getting caught. But even then, they'd be vastly outnumbered. If Pyeong managed to raise the alarm, he and Sadie wouldn't even hear the bullets fire before they landed.

He pushed the worst-case scenario out of his thoughts.

They rode in silence for the rest of the drive. Sadie leaned her head on the window, and when he looked over a few miles later, she had her eyes closed. He wasn't sure if she was asleep, but he wasn't about to disturb her unless he absolutely had to. She'd been through enough.

Unfortunately for them, the worst-case scenario became a reality as soon as they were a mile out from the military base. Bear gently shook Sadie awake. When she turned toward him with sleep still in her eyes, he pointed out the windshield.

Between their car and the entrance to the military base was a line of soldiers aiming automatic weapons at them. Behind the miniature army was a row of vehicles of all shapes and sizes.

"Jesus." Sadie gripped the car door. "The only thing they're missing is a tank."

"I wouldn't be surprised if one rolled up in the next couple minutes."

"We got an escape route?"

Bear checked his rearview mirror. For a second he thought they might get away with slamming on the brakes, whipping the car around, and heading back the way they came. But right as he opened his mouth to suggest the idea, two pairs of headlights burst to life, nearly blinding him in the process.

"That's a negative." He gripped the wheel and turned his attention back to what was in front of them. He started to let off the gas. "Got any ideas?"

She looked down at her map and then back up and out her passenger window. "We're surrounded by trees. And by the looks of it, they're fairly dense. Don't think we'd make it too far."

"Think we can talk our way out of this one?"

She laughed high and tight.

"Right." He pushed down a little harder on the gas. "Won't know until we try."

B ear rolled to a stop about a hundred feet from the line of soldiers. He could hear someone shouting but couldn't make out the words.

Sadie looked over at him. "What are the chances they're just offering us dinner and a movie?"

"Fifty-fifty?" He scratched his chin and then thought better at the sudden movement. "Bet they got snipers on us. We should take this nice and slow."

"Together?" She asked.

He nodded and the two of them slowly opened their doors in tandem. He pulled himself out of the car and stood with his hands raised above his head. Sadie did the same.

The hair rose on the back of his neck. He felt vulnerable. Couldn't stand it. But he reminded himself that if they really wanted to take them out, they would've done it as soon as they had spotted the car. They had enough ammunition to bury the vehicle in a crater.

Bear's ears perked up at the sound of the two cars behind them coming to a screeching halt. Four doors opened and then closed. Guns were racked. Footsteps landed on the asphalt in rhythm. It wasn't until Bear felt the man breathing down his neck that he bothered turning his head to the side.

The man behind him said something in Korean.

"Sorry, buddy. Didn't catch that."

A heavily accented voice came from the other side of the car. "Move forward."

Bear looked over at Sadie, who had two men at her back as well. He nodded his head, and as a unit they moved forward.

He heard the four men following them, their soles scratching against the road. He kept his eyes forward, his brain still scrambling for a way to get out of the situation they were in. But it was hopeless. The only way was through. And they'd be lucky to even get that chance.

The man who spoke in English told them to stop when they were just a few feet from the line. Bear could see the tension in everyone's eyes.

"That's a lot of firepower for just two people," he said.

This time it wasn't the man behind him that spoke, but a figure that emerged from the back of the crowd. Bear wasn't familiar with North Korean uniforms, but it didn't take a native to realize this guy was important. He carried himself like he was untouchable. The general?

"We know of the destruction you and your men left in their wake. In Hong Kong and here in Korea. We want the rest of the team. Where are they?"

Bear threw his head back and laughed so hard he had to wipe the tears from his eyes. When he looked back at the line of soldiers, he noticed the young one in front of him looked spooked.

"There's no team, man. It was just me." He hooked his thumb in Sadie's direction. "She's just a hitchhiker I picked up along the way."

"Hell with you, Bear." Sadie's voice was harsh.

Apparently they were both feeling reckless today.

The officer turned to Sadie. "You were the one that was hired to kill the general."

That answers that question, Bear thought.

Sadie shrugged nonchalantly.

The officer looked at the soldier next to him. "Kill her."

Bear stepped forward at the same time the Korean man did. The sound of weapons being prepared for firing sounded all around him. "You don't want to do that."

The officer looked him up and down and laughed. "Why?"

"Because you need her." Bear wet his lips. He'd gone through a million ways to convince these men they were useful, but none of them were coming to him now. "You need both of us."

"And why is that?"

"She tried to kill him, sure—"

"Not helping," Sadie hissed.

"—But someone hired her, didn't they? Would you rather kill her or would you rather kill the person who gave her the mission?"

"We'd rather kill both," the officer said.

"You don't get both." Sweat trickled down Bear's forehead. It was difficult to play hardball with several dozen automatic weapons pointed at your face. "But I might be able to make it worth your time."

"And how do you plan on doing that?"

"Well, when I say you," Bear said, "I really mean General Pyeong. Is he back there hiding out somewhere?"

The officer's face hardened. "You speak with me. No one else."

"I think the general will want to hear what we have to say."

"And what is that?"

He weighed his options. There weren't many. He decided to be honest. "You tell him that we need to talk about Daniel Thorne."

The officer reacted. No one else. His eyes hardened and then he turned around and made his way back through the crowd who parted wide for him. The men behind Sadie and Bear shoved the barrels of their weapons into their backs once more. The soldiers parted again to let the hostages through.

It looked like Bear had made the right call.

Chapter Thirty-Two

The military base wasn't particularly large, but it was bustling with activity. Everywhere you looked, there were men in uniform. A small group marched in front of Bear, completely in sync with each other. The show of power was impressive, but Bear's thoughts were elsewhere.

He had no idea what kind of person General Pyeong was. Well, other than the kind of person who would kill one brother just to back the other. And if he had gotten into bed with Thorne, that meant he was either extremely gullible or just as ruthless.

Bear was going to place money on the latter option.

Somehow he had to convince Pyeong that the General was one of the loose ends Thorne was trying to tie up. He also had to figure out a way to keep him and Sadie alive in the process. Bear was missing Jack. He was the better bullshitter out of the two of them.

The officer kept them bustling across the compound. Wherever they ran into a group of soldiers, the men would stop and salute. Bear still didn't know who this guy was, but it was clear that even if he wasn't General Pyeong, he was a high-ranking official. Presumably he ran the base when the General wasn't on deck.

Bear and Sadie were led into a concrete building, down several sterile hallways, and finally into an interrogation room. They were placed in a pair of chairs and their hands were handcuffed behind their backs.

The officer left without saying a word, closing the door behind him and leaving them in silence.

"I'm not gonna lie," Sadie said. "I'm not feeling too hopeful here."

Bear looked around the room but didn't spot any cameras. He wasn't sure if that was a good thing or not. On the one hand, that meant no one was listening in. There wasn't any one-way glass either. But on the other hand, that meant there was no security system in the room to hack into.

Not that it mattered. As soon as he'd concocted the plan to rush the military base, any thought of checking in with Neumann had slipped his mind. A rookie move. It would've been more than a little useful to have a pair of friendly eyes on them.

"Really?" Bear turned toward Sadie with a grin on his face. "I was just thinking about how comfortable this room was compared to the hellholes I've heard about."

Sadie shook her head. "Not helping."

He opened his mouth to respond when the door creaked on the other side of the room and a tall, broad, stern-faced man entered. He wore a scowl on his face. A scar snaked its way down from the corner of his right eye to just below his ear. He looked at both Sadie and Bear with a calculated disinterest.

There was no doubt in Bear's mind that this was General Pyeong.

Pyeong looked over his shoulder and nodded. The officer from earlier returned the gesture and closed the door, leaving the general alone with his two guests. Pyeong pulled the chair out from the other side of the table and sat down, hands folded in his lap.

Bear looked over at Sadie. "That was pretty quick. We must be important for the general to hop, skip, and jump his way right over to our comfy little jail cell."

"I feel no need for posturing," the general said. "I hear you know who Daniel Thorne is. I'm interested in hearing what you have to say."

The general's accent was cleaner than the others. It belied an English upbringing. With such a strong sense of nationalism in the country, it was surprising Pyeong had reached a high-ranking position considering he had a British education. Or perhaps that was a testament to the general's tenacity.

Bear pointed his chin in Sadie's direction. "Do you know who this woman is?"

The general glanced quickly at Sadie's face, then back at Bear. "I've been informed that she had tried to orchestrate an attempt on my life. She was unsuccessful."

Bear could feel Sadie rolling her eyes. "Obviously."

"I do have to congratulate you." The general looked at Sadie with the full force of his gaze now. "You've come closer than most in the past few years. Thorne was smart to send a woman. Though not smart enough, it seems."

Bear sat up a little straighter. "So you know it was Thorne who tried to have you killed?"

"I didn't know until you mentioned his name," the general said. "And then a few things clicked into place. It makes sense."

"You seem oddly calm about the idea," Sadie said.

Pyeong shrugged. "One gets used to always being in someone else's crosshairs. You learn to live with the consequences of your power."

Bear leaned forward as far as his bonds would allow. "I can get to him."

"You seem eager to betray your superior. Why should I trust your loyalty to me?"

"He's not my superior. And you shouldn't." Bear leaned back in his chair, trying to look casual with his arms cuffed behind his back. "But you should trust that I want Thorne dead just as much as you do. I'm willing to make that happen. I get him in place and you take him out. Simple as that."

Pyeong was silent for a few seconds. "And what do you expect in return?"

"Let us go." Bear couldn't help the grin that spread over his face. "And don't miss."

Pyeong didn't smile but his eyes lit up. The scene must've played out in his mind's theater. It was the only indication on his face that he liked what Bear had to say. Pyeong pointed to Sadie. "The girl stays."

Bear shook his head. "No deal. We go together."

Pyeong stood up and spread his arms out to the side. "I am not afraid of Thorne. He'll make a mistake eventually, and I'll put a bullet in his brain. I'm a patient man. I don't need you, Mr.—"

"Logan."

"Mr. Logan." Pyeong opened the door and looked back over his shoulder. "But your way is easier, and I'd rather put your life on the line than one of my men's. The girl stays. You'll go. Mao will collect you shortly. I advise you not to disappoint me. I don't offer second chances."

And with that, Pyeong exited the room and closed the door behind him with a sharp *snap*.

Bear had just enough time to reassure Sadie that he'd be back for her before the door opened again. Mao, the officer who had originally taken them to the interrogation room, collected both of them. Sadie was led deeper into the bowels of the base, while Bear was escorted back outside to the car, where it sat in the same place he'd left it.

"You know, you could really work on your people skills," Bear said, folding himself behind the wheel. "Your continued silence is just a little off-putting."

Mao opened the passenger door and got in without a word.

Bear scratched his beard. "The hell are you doing?"

"I've been instructed to ensure Thorne's arrival."

"I think your boss has given me enough incentive to ensure that on my own."

Mao buckled himself in and sat ramrod straight next to Bear. "He doesn't trust that Thorne won't find a way to further manipulate you."

Bear gripped the wheel until his knuckles turned white. "Thorne will get spooked when he finds out I'm not alone. He'll never come out of the shadows."

"Then I suggest you find a way to ensure he does. The general has given you twenty-four hours. If I don't check in every four hours, your friend will be shot in the head." He paused and turned to Bear with a smile on his face. "If she's lucky."

Bear didn't respond. He pulled out the sat phone and called Neumann. "How's everyone?"

"Fine, just fine," Neumann said. "Falcon hasn't returned yet. The old bastard either had a heart attack on his way home or he's waiting for a call to extract you."

Bear groaned. "I told him to go home. I don't need his blood on my hands too."

"You saw how well he listened to me. It's to be expected." There was the clink of a spoon in a teacup in the background. "How's it going for you?"

Bear shot a look at his unwelcome companion. "Found Sadie. She's all right. She's in a bit of a pickle at a military base just over the border. I'm being tasked with locating Thorne, so I'll need you to work some magic."

Bear hoped Neumann understood his subtle request to get some eyes and ears in the military base. Ernie wasn't the best hacker Bear knew, but he was the most readily available at the moment. As long as the systems weren't too complicated, they might have a chance at getting Sadie out of there.

"Copy that." It sounded like Neumann switched the phone from one ear to the other before starting to type something out on his computer. "Anything else?"

"Get ready to set up a camera on Maria."

"Maria? Why?"

Bear didn't like the words that came out of his mouth next, but he also knew they were necessary.

"We may need to use her as bait."

Chapter Thirty-Three

The phone rang ten times before Thorne picked up. The only thing Bear heard on the other end was static. Even when he was silent, Thorne knew how to push Bear's buttons.

Bear grit his teeth. "Thorne."

"Bear." There was relief in Thorne's voice. "I wasn't sure it was you."

Bear could see right through the bullshit, but he played along. "It's been an interesting past couple days."

"Tell me about it." It sounded like he was settling in for story time. "I want to know every detail."

"I'm sure you do." Bear chanced a glance at Mao, who was looking at him with a passive expression on his face. "I found Sadie."

"You did? She okay?"

Bear tried not to let the false interest grind on him. "She's been better. Listen, we need to talk."

"Isn't that what we're doing?"

"In person. Face to face."

Thorne hesitated. "Why?"

"Because I don't trust this line. And I trust you more when I can look you in the eye."

Thorne laughed. "We both know that's a lie."

"Besides, I have something of yours. Goes by the name Maria. Thought you might want her back."

Thorne dropped all pretense. "Is she all right? Where is she?"

"She's safe. For now." Bear let that sink in for a second. "We need to meet. Dandong. Three hours."

"That's awfully short notice. I can't get to China that quickly."

"We both know you wouldn't stay too far away from the action just in case things got interesting and you discovered a way to take advantage of the situation."

"You know me better than I thought you did." Thorne paused a beat. "You have somewhere in mind?"

Bear reached over and grabbed the map from the dashboard. He opened it in his lap and read out the coordinates for a little spot about twenty miles from the base. It looked like there was a small mountain covered in trees. It'd allow Bear to have cover and the high ground.

"See you then."

As soon as Bear hung up, Mao reached into his pocket and pulled out a phone of his own.

"What are you doing?" Bear asked.

Mao ignored him. Bear once again kicked himself for not knowing any Korean. As soon as Mao was done, Bear repeated his question.

"Putting an insurance policy into place. You Americans act like this is the Wild West. It's not. This is the East. This is Korea. I won't let your improvisations cost us the chance at finally getting our hands on Thorne."

"It won't be me who loses him," Bear said. "He's going to smell your men a mile away. He won't show up if the odds aren't in his favor."

"You underestimate me." Mao's voice was sharp. "Do not make that mistake."

"No, I just don't underestimate *him*. You're the one making the mistake here."

Mao remained silent. Bear shook his head and put the car in drive and swung around, heading further East and hoping Sadie would be all right long enough for Bear to survive this death trap.

Mao's men were already in place by the time Bear arrived. He had no idea how they had gotten there before them, but he didn't spend too much time thinking about it. He was too busy taking his frustrations out on Mao.

"This is your plan?" Bear threw his hands up in the air. "It's bad enough you're here, but you expect Thorne not to notice twenty Koreans hiding in the trees?"

Mao didn't respond.

"Will you at least do me the favor of joining your men? If Thorne walks up to the car and sees you, he's going to shoot first and ask questions later."

Mao tucked his phone away and pushed open the door, closing it quietly behind him before disappearing into the trees off to Bear's left.

He didn't spot any movement in the woods, but Bear could practically feel two dozen eyes on him. Thorne was never going to fall for this.

Bear leaned back in his seat and closed his eyes. No point in staying vigilant when the odds were stacked against him at every possible turn. The fog swept in and his mind went numb.

The knock on the window snapped Bear out of sleep. For a

moment he forgot where he was. Back home in the States? On St. Lucia? In Hong Kong? The Philippines? He had been traveling so much over the last week or two that it took him several seconds to remember that he was in North Korea, taking a nap in a stolen vehicle, waiting for the biggest pain in his ass he'd ever met aside from Noble to show up and turn himself in.

But this wasn't a movie, and Bear didn't have that kind of luck.

He looked up at the man standing outside his window, half-expecting it to be Mao wearing a scowl on his face. Instead, it was a white man with a thick brown beard holding a phone up and motioning for Bear to roll down the window.

Bear complied, and the man handed him the phone without a word. As soon as Bear put the cell up to his ear, he was greeted with Thorne's voice.

"You didn't think I'd walk right into that trap, did you, Bear?"

"No." Bear sighed and tried to wipe the sleep from his eyes. "Wasn't my idea."

"I believe it." Thorne chuckled. "How about we meet some place a little more secure?"

"You got somewhere in mind?"

"I do." Thorne was playing up the dramatics. "Do you think you can lose your friends?"

"Won't be a problem."

"Good. My friend there will distract them long enough for you to get away. Feel free to keep the phone. I'm sending the new coordinates now."

Thorne hung up and Bear looked down at the phone in his hand. A few seconds later a text message came in with a series of numbers that would lead him to the new rendezvous.

The man outside the car leaned in close. Bear saw him pull a grenade out of his pocket and remove the pin. "You've got sixty seconds."

Bear didn't hesitate.

He tossed the phone on the passenger side seat, threw the shifter in gear, and slammed his foot down on the accelerator. He wasn't sure if the man was intending to toss the grenade or make it his final act, but he wasn't sticking around long enough to find out.

The patch of woods where Mao's men were hiding was already a sliver of green against the horizon by the time the explosion erupted behind him.

Chapter Thirty-Four

B ear kept the accelerator pressed firmly against the floor until he arrived at the coordinates Thorne had sent. He didn't seem to be followed, but he wouldn't have been surprised if the Koreans had placed a tracker in the car. Or on him, for that matter. He'd get hell for ditching Mao and his men, but it had been the only way to find Thorne.

He hoped Sadie wouldn't pay the price for that stunt.

He jerked on the emergency brake and stepped out of the vehicle into a small field. To the north was a farmhouse. Along with the coordinates, Bear had been instructed to ditch his car and walk up to the front door.

The vast field left him exposed. He had to trust that Thorne still needed him alive. Or at the very least was curious about what Bear had discovered since their last chat.

Before he could knock, the front door to the house opened and Thorne stood there with a grin on his face. Like he knew he was in control and relished it.

Thorne stepped to the side and gestured for Bear to enter. The house was modest and minimal. It didn't seem like anyone else was there, but Bear wouldn't put it past Thorne to have a man or two hiding in a closet upstairs in case things got heated.

"Nice," Bear said. "What'd you do with the previous owners?"

"Paid them handsomely to move out and never come back," Thorne said. "They're vacationing in the South right now."

Bear tried to look casual as he surveyed the room, looking to see if they had any hidden company. "Somehow I doubt that."

"You can relax. We're alone." Thorne seemed to find Bear's actions amusing. "How are you, by the way? How's Jack?"

"Not here to catch up on old times." He felt a fresh sheen of sweat forming on his arms and forehead.

"Fair enough, fair enough. What is it that you needed to talk to me about so desperately?"

Bear turned around so he could see the look on Thorne's face when he spoke. "General Pyeong."

Thorne didn't disappoint. His face showed just the slightest hint of surprise, and that was more than enough.

"You're not as dumb as you look, Bear."

"You're not the first one to make that mistake."

Thorne walked over to the door and peeked out the window before he turned back to Bear. "How much do you know?"

Bear shrugged. "Enough. I know you helped him take out Han Li Choi's brother. You essentially chose which dictator would be sitting on the throne in North Korea."

Thorne waved his hand dismissively. "They were both going to be bad. Han Li just happened to have less of a temper than his brother."

"There are a thousand other solutions that would've—"

"You have no right to preach at me, Logan." There was definite fire in Thorne's voice now. "We both make decisions every day that could change the course of history. Hell, what happened in Costa Rica isn't that different."

Bear laughed. "Not that different? I didn't use the United States' power to back a tyrant."

"Neither did I. The mission was unsanctioned. Completely off the books. Or so I thought."

"That's what this is about, isn't it?" He took a step closer, but he made sure to stay well out of Thorne's reach. He had no idea what kind of weapons the other man had on him. All Bear had was his 9mm and that tiny switchblade. "You got found out."

"Some dumbass intern from Kalamazoo thought he'd be the next choice for Director of the CIA if he did his due diligence cleaning up records in the archive. He wasn't expecting to come across a paper trail that proved we're responsible for one of the world's most cruel dictators."

"If I didn't know better," Bear said, "I'd say you almost sounded sorry."

"It's a good thing you know better then." Thorne started pacing. "Nothing should've been on the books. Not a single note. Not a single receipt. But someone screwed up."

"Other than you?"

"I did my goddamn job." Thorne came to a halt and punctuated his words with a jab of his finger. "I was told to put Han Li in power, so I did. I didn't question it. I didn't hesitate. When it came down to it, Pyeong and I made it happen."

"How did you find out about the intern?"

"Nothing is secret for long these days. Obviously." Thorne went back to pacing. "The intern went to the wrong person, I guess. Or, at least, the right person for me."

"What kind of information did he find?"

"Does it matter? The point is that if the world knew about it, our government's credibility would go out the window."

The picture was starting to come together for Bear. "So you started taking out anyone who was involved in the deal."

"Pyeong is the last piece of the puzzle. Even Han Li doesn't know what we did for him. If I can remove the general from the equation, we're safe again."

"I didn't realize you were such a nationalist."

Thorne looked up sharply. "I might bend the rules whenever I can, Bear, but don't for a second think I don't love my country."

He held up his hands in surrender. "So you thought your perfect solution was to send Sadie after him?"

"It's what she's trained to do."

"After Costa Rica?" He couldn't help the fire building in the pit of his stomach. "You thought it was a good idea to send her out there again?"

"Please, she's stronger than ninety percent of the men we've trained with." Thorne shook his head at Bear. "She had been chomping at the bit. I did her a favor."

The fire in the pit of Bear's stomach erupted. "You nearly got her killed."

"Part of the job."

Bear took a step back from Thorne before he decided to throw a punch. Thorne smiled, like he'd read Bear's mind. He looked Thorne dead in the eye. "Pyeong has Sadie. He said he'll let her go if he gets you."

Thorne paused for a second. "And in what universe did you actually think that was going to work? I respect Sadie and everything she's done, but I'm not giving myself up for her."

"I thought you might say that." Bear pulled out the sat phone and dialed Neumann. "Luckily, I came with my own contingency plan."

Thorne leaned back against the wall with his arms loose at his side, waiting.

He put the phone on speaker and looked Thorne right in the eye. "I'm here with our good pal Thorne. I think he could use a little update on our current situation."

"Copy that," Neumann said. There were some keystrokes in the background. "Tell him to check his email."

Thorne's brow furrowed as he pulled out his phone and swiped at the screen. Bear walked over as soon as he heard the video start to play. It was echoed by the sat phone still in his hand.

The video on Thorne's device showed Maria bound and gagged in the middle of the living room at Falcon's cottage in the Philippines. Bear wondered if she had volunteered to be tied up or if Neumann had to make the decision for her. Either way, there were no tears in her eyes. She sat absolutely still, staring into the camera.

Neumann pulled a gun from off camera and pointed it at her head.

Thorne laughed, but it sounded hollow. Forced. "You wouldn't."

Bear said, "You trained her, Thorne. She's your protégé. The only thing stopping me from putting a bullet in your head is the fact that I need you. I don't need her. If killing her is what will set Sadie free, then I won't hesitate."

"What do you propose?" Thorne asked. He crossed his arms over his chest, the tension in his body tangible.

"You and I return to the military base where you'll turn yourself over to General Pyeong. Sadie and I go free. I never see your pretty face again."

Thorne stared at the video of Maria being held hostage. He licked his lips and looked back up at Bear. "I should've had you murdered instead of that couple."

Bear's body went rigid. It took everything inside him not to react to Thorne's words. The rage blinded him, and for a moment he was only aware of the whoosh of his blood pumping through the veins in his head.

"Go ahead," Thorne continued. "Kill her. She's meaningless to me. Just like Sadie."

Chapter Thirty-Five

Bear saw the shock in Maria's eyes at Thorne's words, but before he could call out the other man's bluff, a sharp alarm sounded from Thorne's phone. He swiped at a notification and a new video popped up on his screen. This one showed two vehicles approaching the house.

They turned toward the window and saw the cars approaching. "We've got company."

Thorne shoved his phone back in his pocket. "Mao's men."

"Bear?" Neumann's voice echoed out of the sat phone. "What's going on?"

"I'll call you back," Bear said, hitting *end* on the call and shoving it in his own pocket. He looked over at Thorne. "Lucky you."

"Lucky us," Thorne replied. "I want to shoot someone, and unfortunately for me, you're still useful."

"What do you think is going to happen here, Thorne? You're at the end of your rope. You're desperate. It's less entertaining than I thought it would be, and more… pathetic."

Thorne opened a closet door and pulled out an AR-15. "We're

at an impasse, my friend. You need me in order to save Sadie. I need you to take out Pyeong so I can wipe my hands clean of this whole mess. We can duke it out after we take care of Mao."

Bear didn't bother arguing. Instead he followed the second car as it circled around the back of the house. "I've got the rear covered."

Thorne didn't answer. He waited for the first car to come to a complete stop before lining up a shot and shooting the windshield. The driver's head whipped back and he slumped over. Blood covered everything behind him. The two doors on the passenger side opened as the men scrambled to get away from the stream of 5.56 NATOs heading their way.

"Don't suppose you have another one of those?" Bear asked.

"Nope."

"Great."

Bear pulled his 9mm out of his waistband and double-checked he had a second magazine on him. When he peered out the back window to see what he was up against, he had just enough time to spot one of the men hefting a grenade in his direction.

"Grenade!"

Bear dove across the room just as the explosion knocked a sizable hole in the wall. He didn't bother looking to see if Thorne had been hit. Didn't even bother waiting for the smoke choking his lungs to clear. He kicked his way through the hole with his pistol at the ready.

All four men in the vehicle had stepped outside the car and were preparing their guns. In the time between when the smoke cleared and the men realized Bear had joined them outside, he managed to get two shots off. The two men closest to him crumpled to the ground, each with a bullet in his chest.

The remaining men ducked for cover behind the car.

Bear sprinted harder. He planted his hand on the still-warm

hood of the car and leaped over it. He came down hard on top of the guy who had thrown the grenade.

Taken by surprise, the man didn't have enough time to react before Bear smashed his face in with the pistol, his forehead split open.

The other guy aimed a shotgun at Bear's head but made a grave mistake. He didn't leave enough distance between them. Bear shoved the barrel out of his face with his hand just as the man fired it. He ignored the pain of his skin burning and squeezed the trigger twice. One round through the guy's neck, the other between his eyes.

Bear didn't wait for the guy to fall before he turned and fired his last shot into the head of the last man. He collapsed back on the ground. The fight was over.

As Bear switched out the magazine, he listened for sounds of gunfire coming from the front of the house. The wind carried voices. That was it. No shouting. No shots echoing. No fighting.

He chose to avoid the confines of the house and circled his way around front. When he neared the northeastern corner of the home, he paused and listened. Nothing. Slowly, cautiously, he peered out from his hiding spot.

Thorne had his back to Bear. Three bodies lay at his feet.

In front of Thorne was Mao, standing stock still with his hands raised above his head. Thorne had his gun pointed there, but the Korean didn't look concerned. He looked defiant.

"You always were a sniveling little brat," Thorne said.

Bear made a beeline for Thorne. Mao either didn't see him or was smart enough not to draw attention to the fact that someone was sneaking up behind Thorne.

"The general is not going to forgive you for this. He will—"

Mao never finished his sentence. Thorne pulled the trigger.

"At least it was quick," Thorne said. It sounded like he was talking to Bear, but he didn't turn around. "He deserved much worse."

Bear stood out of arm's reach from Thorne and aimed his pistol at the man's head. "Drop your weapon."

"Or what? We both know you're not going to shoot me. You need me."

"Do I?" He was beginning to question that himself. "Pyeong wants you in exchange for Sadie. He never said anything about needing you alive."

Thorne chuckled quietly and tossed his gun on the ground. He turned around slowly. "I'm proud of you, Bear. You're not as soft as I thought you were."

"Don't go singing my praises yet." He took a step back to make sure Thorne had no chance of attacking. "I haven't made up my mind yet whether or not I want to shoot you."

"Or maybe you are soft." Thorne's smile disappeared. "If you're gonna do it, then do it. Hesitation makes you look weak." He paused a beat. "Tell me, that couple in the bar on St. Lucia, did Derek know Sophia was pregnant? Or had she decided to wait until after the wedding to clue him in? Kid probably wasn't even his—"

Bear didn't let Thorne finish.

He pulled the trigger and turned away before Thorne's body hit the ground.

Chapter Thirty-Six

Bear was stopped at the same location as the first time he had pulled up to the military base with Sadie. Only this time he wasn't greeted by an entire line of soldiers and vehicles.

General Pyeong and two officers stood alone.

Bear climbed out of the car and rested against it. "A personal visit? I'm honored."

"It's not for you, Mr. Logan." Pyeong looked calm, but Bear could feel the excitement in the air. It diminished somewhat when he noticed Bear was alone. "Where's Mao? And Thorne?"

"Mao and his men didn't make it. It might have to be closed casket for your favorite little soldier." Bear slammed the door shut and turned his back on the general, circling around to the trunk. "As for Thorne, he's right here."

Bear pulled Thorne from the trunk, allowing the man to fall head first to the ground before helping him to his feet. He was bleeding and his hands and feet were bound together, but he was still very much alive.

"I thought about killing him." He watched as Thorne struggled to shuffle forward. Looked like an extra in a zombie flick. "But I couldn't guarantee you would still uphold your end of the bargain."

"Wise of you."

"Where's Sadie?" He made a show of looking around. "Because you don't get him without her."

"Our security system cut out unexpectedly while you were away. Seems she took advantage of the situation."

Bear remained calm. The general was either telling the truth and Neumann had gained access to the military base, or Pyeong was lying and had already killed her.

Bear decided to press the situation. "I call bullshit. Where the hell is she?"

"When she left, I assumed she would've gotten in touch with you. If she's in the wind, maybe she meant more to you than you to her. How disappointing, I'm sure." Pyeong clasped his hands in front of him. "Though, I must admit I'm surprised. I was sure you two would be long gone by now. I sent half my men out looking for you. Imagine my shock when you drove right up to my front gate."

"So that's why I don't get the welcome party this time around, huh? A little understaffed?"

General Pyeong smiled, but it was tight. He reached behind his back and pulled out a pistol. He leveled it at Bear. "I don't need my men to get rid of you, Mr. Logan. I can—"

Pyeong didn't get a chance to finish his sentence. A shot rang out, cutting him off. Bear tensed and felt Thorne do the same. He automatically did a self-check of his body, ensuring that he hadn't missed the fact that he'd been hit. He looked over at Thorne, who appeared to be doing the same thing. They were both unscathed.

Pyeong crumpled to the ground. When the echoes stopped a second shot rang out and the man to the general's right went down. A third shot took out the final officer. Bear grabbed Thorne and retreated to the vehicle.

A figure emerged from the trees off to Bear's left. Their movements indicated that it was a woman. She was carrying a sniper rifle. Even when she was close enough to recognize, Bear had trouble trusting that it was really Sadie.

"Hey, Bear. 'Bout time you showed up." Her easy smile wiped off her face when she turned toward Bear's prisoner. "Thorne."

"Well isn't this a nice twist of fate." Thorne looked at Bear and held up his bound hands. "Maybe this story can have a happy ending after all."

Bear pulled out his pistol and aimed it at Thorne's head. "I'm looking forward to it."

Sadie hefted her rifle and pointed it at Bear. "Don't be stupid. We don't have much time. Pack him up in the car and let's go."

Bear looked down at the weapon aimed at him. "What are you talking about? This is the guy that put you through hell. He put us all through hell. Let's end it. Your mission's over. We don't need him anymore."

"The general was never really my mission," Sadie said. "Thorne was."

Bear couldn't wrap his head around her words. He looked between her and Thorne, who looked just as confused as Bear felt. "Say that again?"

Sadie turned her attention to Thorne and it seemed like she couldn't help basking in his surprise. "It took months of meticulous planning, but here we are. It played out exactly like I thought it would."

Thorne looked her up and down. There was contempt on his face. "Are you delusional? The only reason why you're here is because I played you."

Sadie laughed. "You still think that?" She glanced at Bear. "Did he tell you the story about the intern who found the perfect piece of incriminating evidence in some archive? Did he tell you about how he's been pulling my strings since the beginning, putting this mission in my lap because he knew I wouldn't be able to resist getting back out into the field?"

She took a step closer to Thorne and kept her rifle trained on Bear. "Surprise, Daniel. There was no intern from Kalamazoo. It was me all along."

Thorne was turning red. "What the hell are you talking about?"

"After Costa Rica, I dedicated every day to figuring out who you were." She nodded at Bear. "No offense, but you and Jack were striking out left and right. I decided to take matters into my own hands."

Bear lowered his pistol a couple inches. He was having trouble keeping up. "How?"

"I found every bit of information I could on our good friend Thorne here. Found proof he pulled strings in North Korea." She looked back at their prisoner. "That was a rookie move on your part."

"You couldn't have known that would've led to me."

"That was actually the only thing that I did know going in. Everything else was up in the air. Actually had a helluva time pitching it to my boss. He said I was crazy. Said you're nothing but a myth." She paused a beat. "Then I found proof, and they gave me the green light."

"The sex trafficking ring," Bear said. "The kidnapping?"

"All part of the plan."

"I set that up." Thorne was sputtering now. "I made it so you wouldn't be able to say no."

"You're so predictable." Sadie sounded disappointed, like she had expected better from him. "Worse yet, you're arrogant. I knew you'd find a way to get me to accept that op. Just like I knew you'd find a way to get Bear or Jack involved. But we're not your playthings anymore, Thorne. It's over."

Bear raised his arm again, training the pistol on Thorne's head. "So let's end it. Right here, right now."

Sadie looked a little sad, though she didn't drop her weapon. "I can't let you do that. I respect what you and Jack do. I know that the hard call has to be made sometimes. I know that a bullet can be a thousand times more effective than jail time. But that's not me."

Bear couldn't believe what he was hearing. All they had been through, and now this? "You want him to serve a sentence? He'll get out. You know he will."

Sadie looked right at Thorne when she spoke. "And I'll catch him again. That's my job."

Bear doubted that Sadie would pull the trigger on him even if he did shoot Thorne. Not after everything they had been through. But he saw how much she needed this. Closure. This was her moment, not his.

So he lowered his pistol and took a step back. "Then what's the plan?"

"You stupid bitch." Thorne was trying to move toward her, but all he could do was shuffle. "You have no idea who I am. You have no idea who I know. You have no—"

Sadie didn't let him finish. She took one step forward and brought her knee up into his groin. He let out a grunt and folded forward. She brought the butt of her rifle down across the back of his head. He crumpled to the ground, unconscious.

"Now," she said, a satisfied smile on her face, "maybe he'll shut up for the ride home."

Chapter Thirty-Seven

Thorne remained in the trunk for the duration of their trip across the border. Sadie had insisted on driving, saying she had a much easier way to cross over into China. Bear was fine with that. He spent the majority of their ride staring out the window and trying to process everything Sadie had told him.

After months of looking for Thorne and finally having to lay low because they had been caught in his crosshairs, he'd assumed that Thorne orchestrated everything in order to get Bear to do his dirty work.

Turned out it was Sadie all along. She had made all of them pawns on her chess board in the same way Thorne had all those months ago.

He wasn't angry with Sadie, but he was getting tired of being a cog in a machine that he wasn't in charge of. If he wanted that, he'd still be in the program.

Sadie attempted to strike up a conversation a couple of times, but Bear was so lost in his head, he barely heard her. After a while, she gave up. And before he knew it, she was pulling into the Dandong airport where there were two planes waiting for them.

Bear extracted himself from the car and circled around to the trunk to help Sadie pull Thorne out of his holding pen. When they finally stood him upright, he looked pale and exhausted. Bear couldn't tell if it was from the bullet wound in his shoulder, the knock to the head, or the long car ride in the trunk. Most likely a combination of all three.

"This is it for you, Thorne," Sadie said. "There's no getting out of this now."

Thorne grinned through his pain. "We'll see about that."

Sadie didn't bother responding. She'd already won. She handed him off to two clean-cut guys dressed in black. They dragged Thorne toward one of the planes.

Bear pointed at the retreating figures. "What is all this?"

"The CIA came through." Sadie shrugged like that explained everything. "Look, Bear—"

He held up a hand. "You don't have to apologize."

"I know." Sadie's eyes were hard for a split second, but then they softened. "And I'm not. Kind of."

"That makes sense. Kind of."

She placed a hand on his shoulder. "I'm not going to apologize for finding a way to capture Thorne. And I won't apologize for not killing him. This was the right play, from start to finish."

"So then what are you apologizing for?"

"Getting you mixed up in all of this." She crossed her hands over her chest and looked back at Thorne. "I knew what he was going to do. I knew he'd drag either you or Jack into this mess. I didn't want that to happen, but it was the only way to keep him distracted. If he was too busy watching you guys, then he wouldn't have enough time to keep a close eye on me."

"You were hoping it was gonna be Jack, weren't you?"

Sadie smiled softly. "Maybe a little bit. But to be honest, I'm kind of glad it was you. Jack would've made a mess out of this entire situation."

"You're not wrong." Bear looked over at Thorne, who was struggling against his captors. It appeared that he didn't want to go up the stairs and into the plane. Maybe he knew it truly would be the end of him. "What about Maria?"

"Who?"

"Maria, the girl Thorne had trained. The one who took the fall for you. The one who nearly got killed."

"We only found out about her when Thorne put her into play." Sadie's nostrils flared and her cheeks darkened. "That wasn't my call. I didn't want her to take the fall for me. I didn't want her to go through what she did just to have me get even closer to the general."

"She's a good kid," he said. "And she could use a better mentor than Thorne."

"I'll keep that in mind. I don't know if I can swing it. At the very least my superiors are gonna want to question her. There are a lot of things Thorne needs to answer for. Things we weren't privy to in Costa Rica. She'll be part of bringing him down, whether she wants to or not."

"I wouldn't count her out just yet. Thorne was more than willing to let me put a bullet in her head before he gave himself up. She's gonna feel some type of way about that."

Sadie raised an eyebrow. "A bullet in her head?"

"I wasn't actually going to do it." He placed a hand on Sadie's shoulder and was silent for a moment. "Are you okay?"

"A bit bruised still, but that'll fade. I'll be fine, don't worry about me."

"Oh, I'm not worried about you," he said. "If anything, I'm worried about me. With you back out on the streets, who knows what could happen."

Sadie laughed and reached for his hand. "I promise I won't get you into any more trouble. For what it's worth, thank you. For finding me, for helping me. For trusting me when I said I wanted to do this the right way."

He nodded and said nothing.

A shout from across the hangar grabbed both of their attention. Bear turned to see Thorne still struggling with his captors, though they'd made it to the top of the stairs.

Sadie started walking in Thorne's direction, Bear at her heels.

"What's the problem?" Sadie called out.

Thorne immediately stopped struggling. "You never answered my question from earlier, Bear. I need an answer."

"I'm done playing by your insane rules." Bear held up his hand, his middle finger extended. "That's the only answer you'll get from me. Fuck you."

"Put him on the damn plane already," Sadie said. She started leading Bear toward the other one, which he presumed was there to take him wherever he needed to go.

"But I want to know. I have to know." Thorne was manic now. "You never answered me earlier today. How's Jack?"

Bear stopped short. He twisted his neck to get one more look at Thorne.

The man was laughing hysterically now. His grip on reality was slipping. He held on to the rail long enough to settle himself down. Then between ragged breaths he said one last thing.

"Have you heard from him lately?"

THE END

Bear will be back to deal with Thorne in the 3rd Bear Logan novel in 2019.

Until then, catch up on Noble & Bear's adventures in the Jack Noble series - Links for all books below!

Want to be among the first to download the next Jack Noble

book? Sign up for L.T. Ryan's newsletter, and you'll be notified the minute new releases are available - and often at a discount for the first 48 hours! As a thank you for signing up, you'll receive a complimentary copy of *The Recruit: A Jack Noble Short Story.*

Join here: http://ltryan.com/newsletter/

I enjoy hearing from readers. Feel free to drop me a line at ltryan70@gmail.com. I read and respond to every message.

If you enjoyed reading *A Deadly Distance*, I would appreciate it if you would help others enjoy these books, too. How?

Lend it. This e-book is lending-enabled, so please, feel free to share it with a friend. All they need is an amazon account and a Kindle, or Kindle reading app on their smart phone or computer.

Recommend it. Please help other readers find this book by recommending it to friends, readers' groups and discussion boards.

Review it. Please tell other readers why you liked this book by reviewing it at Amazon, Barnes & Noble, Apple or Goodreads. Your opinion goes a long way in helping others decide if a book is for them. Also, a review doesn't have to be a big old book report. If you do write a review, please send me an email at ltryan70@gmail.com so I can thank you with a personal email.

Like Jack. Visit the Jack Noble Facebook page and give it a like: https://www.facebook.com/JackNobleBooks.

Also by L.T. Ryan

The Jack Noble Series

The Recruit (free)

The First Deception (Prequel 1)

Noble Beginnings

A Deadly Distance

Ripple Effect (Bear Logan)

Blowback (Bear Logan)

Thin Line

Noble Intentions

When Dead in Greece

Noble Retribution

Noble Betrayal

Never Go Home

Beyond Betrayal (Clarissa Abbot)

Noble Judgment

Never Cry Mercy

Deadline

End Game

Mitch Tanner Series

The Depth of Darkness

Into The Darkness

Deliver Us From Darkness - coming soon

Affliction Z Series

Affliction Z: Patient Zero

Affliction Z: Abandoned Hope

Affliction Z: Descended in Blood

Affliction Z Book 4 - Spring 2018

About the Author

L.T. Ryan is a *USA Today* and international bestselling author. The new age of publishing offered L.T. the opportunity to blend his passions for creating, marketing, and technology to reach audiences with his popular Jack Noble series.

Living in central Virginia with his wife, the youngest of his three daughters, and their three dogs, L.T. enjoys staring out his window at the trees and mountains while he should be writing, as well as reading, hiking, running, and playing with gadgets. See what he's up to at http://ltryan.com.

Social Medial Links:

- Facebook (L.T. Ryan): https://www.facebook.com/LTRyanAuthor

- Facebook (Jack Noble Page): https://www.facebook.com/JackNobleBooks/

- Twitter: https://twitter.com/LTRyanWrites

- Goodreads: http://www.goodreads.com/author/show/6151659.L_T_Ryan

Printed in Great Britain
by Amazon

37340602R00138